THE CONSPIRATORS

It had happened once before, at Palomares, and now it had happened again. A wrong weather report, a plane crash in the fog, and an American bomb released on the Devon coast. Of course they'd cleaned up the mess, and with total efficiency, but in Spain there'd been a second bomb which the Americans hadn't admitted until events had simply forced them to. That had been a bad mistake, the sort of thing people would remember. The Burke Hoe crash was just plain bad luck, but it could easily be made to sound both negligent and sinister.

Charles Russell was no scientist, but he was no fool either. He knew there was no danger whatever of a nuclear explosion at Burke Hoe. But a political explosion there could well be—would be, if any rumours were allowed to escape into the wrong hands. There were extremists of both right and left who would like nothing better than a crisis in Anglo-American relations, and this was a loaded gun in their hands. It was Charles Russell's job to make sure that the gun could never be fired.

THE

WILLIAM HAGGARD

CONSPIRATORS

Walker and Company • New York

First published in the United States of America
in 1968 by Walker and Company, a division of
Walker Publishing Company, Inc.

Library of Congress Catalog Card Number:
68-13441.

Printed in the United States of America from
type set in Great Britain.

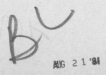

Relations between the United States and Britain are strained when a U.S. plane loses an atomic bomb off the coast of Devon. Although the Americans are successfully recovering the bomb it is rumored that, as in Spain, there is another bomb somewhere, unacknowledged.

Martin Dominy was watching them clear up the mess, thinking they did it efficiently since they'd had previous practice at clearing up messes. They'd dropped a couple in Spain at a place called Palomares. Neither bomb had exploded, but the licking of anti-American chops had been as noisy as a nuclear bang and politically almost as damaging. And here at Burke Hoe they'd contrived to drop another. There was only one this time and it was square on the beach. There were no complications with a second in deep water.

There was only one this time, they'd insisted on it officially.

Dominy watched on, impressed. The little bay was stiff with shipping—some sort of supply ship, tenders, two frigates, a constant coming and going of busy launches. The beach had been wired off behind a cordon of British police, and behind them again, discreetly inconspicuous, were armed men, not British. Round the bomb itself they'd built a sort of wooden shed. That had been done two days ago, within hours of the actual incident, by a detail of Marines which had dropped from the sky in choppers. Now they were ready to move it. Huge crawling catskinners had cleared a path through the rocks to the beach itself and over the wooden shed stood a crane on tracks. They were ready to go and they'd hoist it when the ship came. The tank-landing craft would slide into the beach stern first, her ramp would drop to expose her enormous maw, the crane would lift, then move down the combat landing strip . . .

And that would be the end of it. Except that of course it couldn't be.

I

Martin Dominy was on the cliff with the reporters, a thoroughly British compromise. Kept at a distance they couldn't be nuisances, but they could watch and they were doing so. One even had a radio and through a relay could call his newsroom. Martin turned to the man beside him, a reporter from the *Gong*; he knew him slightly privately and admired his public competence; he asked him now:

'What do you make of it?'

'I make them bloody good at it.' The reporter put his binoculars up, reviewing the teeming beach. 'Just imagine how we'd be handling that. There'd be sailors stumping about and blowing whistles, soldiers shouting. The sailors would be up-stage of course, resenting the soldiers and showing it. There'd be a great deal of noise and more brass caps than useful men. But what they've got there is a working navy. They don't clutter their wardrooms with portraits of that admiral and they don't call soldiers Brown Jobs. They don't do either because they don't need to. They're not in decline so they're not defensive. They're a top-line outfit and you can take them as you find them. As you find them, not as grandpa did.'

Martin Dominy laughed. 'I know what you mean but it wasn't what I was asking you. I meant where do they go from here?'

'I'd guess back to a New England port. The buzz is that the tank-landing craft should be here in an hour and a half at most, then they'll load the bomb and take it with them. They'll ship that splendid machinery too.' He pointed at the wooden shed. 'And pull that down. Finally they'll roll the wire.' He waved at the bay. 'Look at those ships, I make it ten. But six hours from now there won't be one. If you wanted to bathe you could use the beach.'

Martin asked thoughtfully: 'You really mean that?'

'You're thinking of radiation? Phooey. There's a man here

2

with a Geiger and he's been listening. All he's been getting is a chatter from the night dial on his wristwatch. Of course we're too far to rely on that, it must be a couple of hundred yards, and the fact that they've stated publicly that nothing is leaking means equally nothing. They said that too in Spain. At first. But they took away soil by the ton a few days later. I wouldn't believe a word they said—why the hell should I when whatever they say they're told to? But I do believe my eyes.' The reporter waved at the beach again. 'You think they'd be walking about in ordinary clothes if a risk existed? They'd be muffled up like spacemen, they take radiation seriously.'

'You believe what they've put out then?'

'I believe there's no radiation. I do believe that part.'

'And the rest?'

'What rest?'

'That they dropped only one bomb.'

The reporter said deliberately: 'Out in the Bristol Channel there's some fairly deep water, deeper in places than the continental shelf off Palomares. I'm told that between here and Lundy Island there are pockets far beyond the current Deep Submergence Systems. That proves nothing no doubt—it's a negative inference. But if that aircraft was carrying more than one bomb it could easily have gone somewhere where the tempting thing would be to say that it never existed. Picking up a bomb from a beach is child's play, even diving for it at reasonable depths is the sort of technical exercise they might welcome as practice. Not that they're not good at it by now. But if it's really in deep water the first thing I'd do would be deny that it was anywhere. Come to that, why are *you* here? I know who employs you.'

'I'm damned if I know,' Martin Dominy said.

He hadn't expected to be believed but the man from the *Gong* accepted it. 'Charles Russell sent you down on spec?'

'That's what it looks like.'

It was true, Martin thought: Russell's instructions had for once been imprecise. Martin Dominy was to go down to Burke Hoe and there keep his eyes open. A member of the aircraft's crew was alive still but only just, and though they might not let him see him he should check on his condition with the local hospital. Finally since she happened to be living there, he was also to look Casilda up.

The little beach had been enclosed, but there was a single gate in the rolls of barbed wire. It was guarded by stolid North Devon police and from time to time a man in American uniform would come to it. The journalists took it in turns to attend his appearances, indifferent and sceptical. What they were getting were handouts and they knew it; they knew equally well that the real story lay thousands of miles distant from the wire which was excluding them. A nuclear bomb had been jettisoned from an aircraft which had broken up. They could see the hut which screened it. It didn't seem to be leaking dangerously—they could see that also. These were facts and a bare story, already headlines in the Press of half the world, but the why and how, the follow-up, lay in Germany where the flight had begun or in America where the aircraft had been directed.

Amongst the waiting men there was a moment's stir as an American officer again approached the gate, a stir of boredom broken rather than of real anticipation. The bomb would be taken away and that would end it. It would end it at Burke Hoe, at least. They could all go back to London and the lucky ones be sent on elsewhere, to the States perhaps or Germany, to the story, the real one.

And by God there was going to be one.

At the barrier in the wire the attendant reporter waited. The officer came up to him, said something, saluted politely. The journalist made a note of it, then walked back up the path to the cliff and his friends. He didn't hurry, he didn't shout, and only a few men met him. But the word seeped down the line of waiting men: the tank-landing craft was on schedule, it would all be over in hours at most. An accident, highly regrettable, but the officer had no comments on that. There were officials in Grosvenor Square whose job it was, and privately the Captain thanked his God for it.

Martin Dominy looked at his watch. The ship would be in in an hour and a half and he might as well watch the landing. Meanwhile he'd been given a job to do and an hour and a half would cover it. Charles Russell had told him to call on Casilda Paine-Pelling. She was the widow of one of his colleagues in the Executive and he'd more than once wondered how long she would remain so. He put away his binoculars, rising stiffly. He'd use the odd hour to pay his duty call.

In the Security Executive Colonel Charles Russell had been reading the morning newspapers. They were very much part of his normal day and usually they were clipped for him, but in moments of trouble he took them as they came in. And Burke Hoe was potentially trouble. Three hours' steady reading had depressed him, for with twenty years' experience he could assess the situation. The business of the Security Executive was the security of the nation, and the phrase was interpreted loosely. It caught spies when it was asked to since it had resources not available to better-publicized organizations, but this would be a chore to be accepted only when other and highly competent bodies had failed and had invited help. The Executive's bread and butter was in the penumbra of dubious politics, the half-world where a respected name was well known to be a Communist but would have won enormous damages if any newspaper had dared say so. All Fleet Street would know, Charles Russell knew; if the man was a Member, as one certainly was, it was also highly probable that the

Cabinet knew as well. But this was an open society still, the rule of law still paramount. Hence the Security Executive.

Russell sighed gently. It was part of his terms of reference that he was seldom given orders even orally; he could be disowned and disgraced and at sixty he was inured to it. There'd be somebody else's hat on the bentwood hatstand but it was unlikely the Executive would be abolished. It was very much too useful to its masters across Whitehall. So a bland voice could telephone, inviting him to a casual drink, or a briskly businesslike young secretary would call him for ten-thirty and make it sharp. Russell couldn't hope for precise instructions and would have regarded it as improper, even as in its way unfair, to have asked for them in terms, but there would be the sort of understanding which best expressed itself in silences. That is, if they did send for him. That bomb was a hot potato and they had plenty of those already.

Charles Russell knew just how hot and why. Because putting it at the most charitable it was unfortunate to jettison nuclear weapons on other people's territory, especially when you'd done it once before. Whichever way you looked at it that was something to be avoided, but nothing had exploded and it seemed established there was no leakage. So the quick clean-up they were so good at, then apology and assurances.

Alas, it might not end like that. America was one of two Great Powers and it was part of her policy to keep nuclear weapons in Europe. You might like it or you might not but you couldn't have it both ways. You couldn't, for instance, give a military aircraft flight-clearance, then complain when she tore herself to pieces in a storm, a killer front which the met. men had underestimated. Logically her cargo had been irrelevant, but people weren't always logical and newspapers hardly ever. Russell picked up one solidly Centre and it was decidedly more than caustic, and when the weekend prestige Press came out there'd be a part of it, both Right and Left, which would foam at the mouth in self-righteous rage. It detested America and all things American. So that pack would go screaming off again, hunting its never acknowledged hare, the end of the American connection. Dropping a bomb on the Devon coast . . .

A bomb? *But there'd been two before.* Suppose there'd been a second one, suppose it was even believed there had. No newspaper had dared assert it yet, nobody had yet called a United States Ambassador a liar. The formal denial stood but on the record that meant little. Proof of a single bomb then? But what proof? The aircraft's papers were lost with the plane itself. Sworn statements from her loaders, some public inquiry with the man who commanded the airfield swearing blind that there'd only been one? That would all count for nothing if a rumour got firmly rooted. If a second bomb had in fact been dropped where it was presently irrecoverable it would be natural, even inevitable, for its existence to be denied. Charles Russell didn't suspect it had but he was accustomed to handling evidence and evidence must be positive. But nine out of ten had a different habit—not was there a second bomb, but could there be. It hadn't been proved there wasn't and in Spain once before . . .

Well, my dear think for yourself, and yes, old boy, it does look fishy. A few million people believing that and almost anything could happen. Not unreasonably, give them their due. God knew how many megatons were lying in the Bristol Channel. Radiation, a killing sea. Or the thing went up and the waters with it. Cardiff and Newport vanished. Anything might happen if that poison really bit, a great deal more than a casual strain on relations with America which an odd misalliance of Right and Left would like to destroy or at least emasculate.

But a pressure group was one thing, reality another. There was an emotional anti-Americanism which Russell and many

7

more despised, but there were other men too, their ultimate ends defined and clear. Their means might have changed in recent years, their basic objective never.

Charles Russell pulled his grey moustache. He couldn't foresee the future but he had half a lifetime of experience. What would he do himself if he were a policy-maker in an international organization dedicated to the disruption of a system which it sincerely considered immoral? Thirty years ago and the question would have been unanswerable, since dropping a bomb on the coast of North Devon wouldn't have fitted comfortably into a dogma of proletarian revolution, preferably by means of war. Today the canon was more sophisticated, Anglo-American relations a perfectly logical target for a communist. They could hardly survive a bomb abandoned, they might barely survive a belief that one had been. There was motive here and an opening too. There were also the men to use it. Sow suspicion and water it; seize on some coincidence and puff it into relevance; harp on the uncertainty, the negative might-be, the dreadful unknown. It wasn't what people knew which made them tick; it was what they feared.

Charles Russell tapped the solid desk thoughtfully. He had already put his machine into the first of its several gears. He'd sent Dominy to Burke Hoe with a roving commission: he was to keep his eyes wide open and to report at once if he saw anything unusual. But he had telephoned already that he had not—only the deadly, the shaming efficiency of the United States Navy. He'd been shown a collection of photographs too, told to telephone at once if he saw any of the faces. But he hadn't and had reported so. Burke Hoe was the end of nowhere, not the likely home of a serious agent, so if they hadn't sent one in and it seemed they hadn't . . . True, a party member lived there but Russell didn't take her seriously. For one thing she carried a party card, and it was the experience of the Executive that anything of importance was seldom entrusted to card-carriers. There was a core of trained activists, controlled from the top, and Russell had files on all of them. He owned a list of members too, not fully up-to-date perhaps, but its acquisition had been invaluable. So Bridget Deshmukh was on this list and some notes, short of a proper file, about her background. She wasn't an Indian but an Irishwoman married to one. Born Bridget Macnamee and for Russell's taste too conscious of it. Grandfather shot in the Troubles—she hadn't forgotten. A nurse in the hospital up the coast at Farracombe. Hardly the calibre for a serious operation, and if they hadn't sent in another man . . .

Russell sighed again quietly. It looked all right, he sensed it wasn't.

Martin Dominy had been lying on the cliff and now rose stiffly. The stiffness soon passed for he was in enviable physical shape, a solidly made man in his early thirties. He went swinging his walking stick, the badge of rank of operators in the Executive. It wasn't a swordstick and it hid no kind of firearm. Martin Dominy had been comprehensively trained; he could shoot and fight dirty, he could look after himself; but fancy weapons he despised as his instructors had frankly mistrusted them.

He had drifted into the Executive from the Civil Service which he had hated. Drifted, he reflected now, smiling a wide uncynical smile, was about the worst word which could conceivably have occurred to him. Nobody drifted into the Executive, but nor were they recruited openly. It was useless to apply: half the romantic misfits of his age and type had tried and never got near the place. But somehow you could get there. You could, that is, if Charles Russell approved you.

Martin's own case had in one sense been typical. He'd been a Principal in the Home Office and had thoroughly disliked it—the caution and the precedents, the law-clotted costive mess. After a year or two he'd asked for an interview with the Principal Establishment Officer. If a transfer could be arranged . . .

The P.E.O. rubbed a well-shaven chin. He liked Martin Dominy and privately he sympathized. Martin had virtues but they weren't the Civil Service ones; he took decisions too easily—he liked to take decisions; he was friendly and un-pompous, and protocol drove him crazy; he laughed easily and too often and he'd always see people as people, never as files. Finally he weighed thirteen stone and if he was still at a desk at fifty he'd weigh a ton.

The P.E.O. had recently had a confidential letter, and now he weighed Dominy against the requirements it had set out. He would rather lose a tooth than staff, especially when efficient, and though Martin might be unhappy he did his job. The P.E.O. reflected. He was a Companion of the Bath but he knew that he had missed things. Martin was young and he liked the man.

The P.E.O. dismissed him without decision, for he hadn't reached Under Secretary rank by saying yes across a table, but a fortnight later Martin was attending what was evidently a selection board at an organization which contrived to be both hush-hush and very well known. He had realized they had liked him but he hadn't liked their smell at all. There'd been the same stale stink of protocol, of seniority, of what was done. He'd had a letter of invitation but had turned it down unhesi-tatingly.

And that, he had thought, was the end of that: he'd stay in a chair and he'd rise within reason. Not to the top since he wasn't equipped to reach it, but he knew he was efficient and he'd go to Assistant Secretary. But it hadn't been the end—not quite. He knew by now that the organization he had said no to had connections and close ones with several others. Someone, he surmised, had talked, discreetly passing his name on. He was guessing that still because he'd never cared to ask it, but he'd been lunching at his club one day and a friend had come up to his table.

'You've heard of Charles Russell?'

'Of course. Who hasn't?'

'You know him?'

'I wish I did.'

'He'd like to buy you a glass of port wine. The library when you've finished.'

That had been five years ago and all of them had been interesting. There'd been training, then odd assignments. Then assignments even odder. Martin Dominy was happy though he wasn't yet very senior.

He wasn't yet very senior but his prospects were rather better than he knew. Russell was sixty and astonishingly active, but at sixty the wise administrator gave some thought to the succession. He had three chief assistants and all of them were excellent since they wouldn't have lasted a day if they'd been otherwise. But somehow he didn't see any as quite crown prince. His world was alarmingly complicated and daily becoming more so, the changing channels, the shifting rocks, the almost daily nuances as a conflict at bottom changeless moved from freezing cold to almost warm. He knew that this was tactics at most, the grand strategy quite uncompromised, but Charles Russell was a pragmatist and when it grew warm he would welcome the sun. He'd keep watching the horizon too, since one day the freeze could come again. But who would have thought three years ago that he could telephone east sixteen hundred miles and talk to a colleague freely? On some things, that is: on others, never. But there was sometimes ground in common and when there was that he'd work on it. This didn't much look like common ground—far from it. Even if it had been someone must use that telephone when his own time came to go, and he couldn't see any assistant doing

11

that. Not quite and not easily. They were admirable officials, far from inflexible, but something more was needed when you were getting away with murder, the unfakable spark of sympathy which set another man alight for you. The three chief assistants lacked it.

Martin Dominy then? Charles Russell had considered it. Not yet of course, very possibly never, but the boy did have brains and a certain grace. That was the word, a certain grace. You made it look easy even if you stayed up all night to do so. That mightn't be fashionable, the plodder was unchallenged king, but in the higher flights of security it was how you did it which finally counted, not what you did. This business at Burke Hoe was a case in point.

It could be if it developed as Russell feared it would.

So Martin walked up the hill to the upper town. Burke Hoe in effect was a town at two levels beside the bay, the lower a watering place, deader than a desert for nine months of the year but now in high summer active. There were cafés and rows of bathing huts, boarding houses and a car park. Down the coast there was even a fun fair. It wasn't Martin's taste for a seaside break. The noise was incessant, the car park packed. There were holiday-makers but gawpers too, standing six deep along the newly laid barbed-wire fence. They stared and they chattered and some just stared. Moving them on was hopeless—the police hardly tried. Move one lot and another came. Burke Hoe was having its day of fame.

Martin climbed on to the upper town, if town, he thought, was a just description. This was where the natives lived, in bungalows and a villa or two, mostly broken into flats. Three hotels trying hard. It was neither cheerful nor cosy and in winter must be the end of all. Martin shuddered though the sun was warm, but he'd been told to pay a formal call on the widow of a colleague. Casilda Paine-Pelling—ridiculous name.

He found her flat at last in one of the grimmer villas. It was

12

a conversion as most others were and he went up the outside staircase. He rang and nobody answered. He rang again.

Odd. The windows were open, and with all those strangers a mile away no sensible housewife would go shopping and leave windows open. Besides, there was milk on the doorstep still.

Martin Dominy tried the flat below. This too was shut, but decently, its windows closed. He went up again thoughtfully. The outside staircase hugged the wall of the house diagonally, ending blankly in the door to the upper flat. He couldn't see through the fanlight and tried a shout. No answer again. He tried the door. Locked.

He was conscious of a sensation he'd known before. There were a dozen valid reasons why a woman should be out, even if it was careless to leave windows quite so invitingly. There were a dozen valid reasons but he didn't quite credit any of them. Instead, very slightly, he'd started to sweat. He felt in his pocket. His training had included certain basic skills with doorlocks and the lock was old and in any case cheap. He broke it in ninety seconds flat.

There was a vestibule first, then a door into the living-room. He opened it. Across the length of the room was a low divan. Casilda Paine-Pelling was sprawled on it, half on, half off.

For a moment he thought her dead.

13

CHAPTER TWO

Charles Russell had been lunching with Lord Normer of Nowhere. This wasn't his style and title but it had stuck. He was a scientist who had properly been ennobled for outstanding work in science, but he hadn't fancied a territorial title derived from territory he had never held. So, since he'd been born there, he had suggested Lord Tooting Bec. This hadn't gone down well. For one thing there had been a music-hall song about Tooting Bec—an elderly Herald could remember it verbatim—and for another Tooting wasn't considered euphonious. The future peer was a first-class scientist but hardly an enthusiast for the niceties of nobility. He had told them to toss up for it and presumably somebody had. He had a handle now but it amused him to forget it. He was Normer of Nowhere and secretly rather proud of it. No feudal halfwit bore arms as ancient.

More important to Charles Russell he was a scientist with an uncommon gift; he could explain things to laymen simply, despising ill-digested chatter about two cultures. He was Russell's guide and compass into a world which he hadn't been trained for. At the moment he held a quart of beer. He had a beer-drinker's stomach but was happily resigned to it; he was saying unbeerily:

'You give me the facts and I'll try and comment usefully.'

'There aren't very many which haven't been in the newspapers. The Americans decided to bring back a nuclear bomb from Europe. Now why should they do that?'

'I can't give you an answer, or not for certain. Perhaps it had gone dicy.'

'Dicy?'

'Why not?' Lord Normer took a swig of beer. 'But you must remember that I'm not a nuclear physicist, I'm a radar man, an expert they tell me though I'm modest enough to doubt it, so I'm not really telling you more than any competent scientist could give you a line on. But look at a hydrogen bomb itself. It's immensely inert. There was never the slightest danger in Spain that anything would go off bang. The danger was radiation—you could say that the insulation had failed, or at least that the failure was partial. But we know that hasn't happened at Burke Hoe. For one thing they've said so, and it would be a terribly risky lie if it wasn't true; and for another they'd be wearing protective clothing, hosing the beach like crazy if suspicion even existed. So radiation's out and so's a bang.'

'You're sure of the latter?'

'I'm pretty sure. If you found a hydrogen bomb in your garden you could picnic on it quite cosily.'

Charles Russell said dryly: 'I doubt if I'd want to try it.'

'I suspect you might be right at that—the theory is one thing, the practice another. The core of a hydrogen bomb is naturally hydrogenous. It'll be deuterium oxide possibly, heavy water in ordinary language, or maybe tritium oxide, which is double heavy water, though it needn't be all that wet. It doesn't explode, it can't explode. It *im*plodes on itself and releases heat and energy. Fantastic, appalling quantities, but there's only one thing which will set it off and that's an old-style atomic bomb.'

'Which you fire with a charge of conventional explosive.'

'Just so.' Lord Normer grinned. 'So maybe you'd be wise in your layman's way about that picnic.'

'Three parts to the bomb,' Charles Russell said.

'That's what I meant by dicy.'

'Expound.'

15

'I can't—not with authority. It's not my line. But I've heard that the business end of a hydrogen bomb can deteriorate. Not always, I gather, but it's known that stocks are checked. It would be simple madness not to.'

'And there's the atomic part too, and the conventional primer.'

'You may not be a scientist, Charles, but you think extremely logically.'

'I thank you for the compliment.' There was a reflective pause. 'So an inspector of bomb stocks—let's call him that—does a routine check and spots a suspect. Naturally he'd send it home.'

Lord Normer considered it. 'Not quite so naturally.'

'Why not?'

'If it was something he'd seen before he might not bother. He might even know the answer on the spot. But if it was something new, something *generic*——'

'You mean the defect could be repeated in other bombs?'

'Precisely. Then he'd certainly order it home to the back-room boys.'

'Reverting to the facts, if I may——'

'You know something the papers don't?'

'Not quite that. But I deduce the job was done in a tearing hurry. Stocks of bombs are changed over, that's more or less common knowledge, but they're changed as you would expect, by regular flights in the same type of aircraft which brought them in. But this was done hurriedly and in some sort of freighter. It wasn't flying a bomber's route and in any case it was miles off course. It had trouble with the weather, then chose wrong. There'll be an interminable wrangle about the met. advice we gave her, but the fact remains that she broke herself up.'

'The crew was inexperienced?'

'I wouldn't think so for a moment. But it wouldn't surprise

me if they'd never carried a bomb before. It also wouldn't surprise me if she was uncomfortably near her maximum load. I'm as ignorant of aeroplanes as I am of nuclear weapons, but aircraft fly over weather if they can possibly contrive to.'

Lord Normer said thoughtfully: 'And one of the crew's alive still.'

'But only just. He came down on a parachute a mile or two from Burke Hoe. It was blowing every which way and he smashed himself up badly. He was lucky a poacher found him. He's in hospital at Farracombe and they're not certain that he'll live. Anyway, he's unconscious still.'

'It might be better if he died.'

'For the Americans? I take the point.'

There was another considerable silence which Normer broke; he said at length: 'I can guess your next question.'

'It's obvious, isn't it? They were carrying a bomb and you used the word generic. So we've a defect in a bomb which might well be affecting other bombs.'

Lord Normer nodded.

'You're a scientist, you'd like to check. Would one be enough, a single sample?'

'Perhaps.'

'But you'd prefer to have others—the more to check the better? Two's better than one in any experiment?'

'Of course.'

'That's what I feared.' Charles Russell said.

He walked back to the Executive, sorting out his thoughts. There wasn't a shred of evidence that another bomb had been put on board but Lord Normer had given a reason why a second could in fact have been. And if that had really happened it was now in the Bristol Channel. That put it much too simply though—Charles Russell wished it didn't. It wasn't immediately relevant that a bomb might be in the deep blue sea: what was relevant inescapably was that people might start to think there

17

was, perfectly ordinary people, normally a-political. People might be *made* to think, a frightening number of people.

Back at his desk he put the situation against its background. His country had lost an Empire, accepting instead a Commonwealth which in terms of real power was impotent. The thing was a burden, a gilding of a declining sun. Europe? They didn't seem to think much of us there and in Russell's view very sensibly. A certain understanding with America was all we had. It had taken some knocks from time to time but had survived on mutual interest—just. There'd been embarrassments before and they'd probably be repeated. There could certainly be another if all the stops were pulled out on this matter of dropping a bomb on the sacred soil. Not that that mightn't be manageable. Whoever was Prime Minister would have to fly off to the States again, assuring his country's protector (Russell flinched at the word but accepted it philosophically) that despite the antics in certain quarters he was still in the saddle firmly, that his heart was still in the same right place, that policy was unchanged, unbent . . .

He'd done it before and had so far got away with it. But perhaps not for ever since the patience of great patrons was notoriously exhaustible.

Russell heard himself swear and it was something he did seldom. He walked to the mirror, an elegant country Chippendale, his private property. He looked the same—six feet and trim still, no nonsense about a body belt. All his own hair, a healthy skin, an exceptionally active, an exceptionally well-preserved man in late middle age. Just the same he had sworn and he hadn't meant to do so.

He had sworn on a reflex, not at men he thought unrealistic. They mattered less than they thought, but people mattered, just ordinary unintellectual men and women. Get enough of those believing that there might be another bomb offshore and it wouldn't be a case of a Prime Minister stroking Mr

President's whiskers. To start with he wouldn't have time for the trip; he'd be up against the wall and fighting hard, fighting for his political life which Russell wouldn't be interested in, and fighting to block some action which could leave his country isolated, some crazy hasty insult which no principal Power could forgive or forget. In terms of internal politics the pressure might break a Prime Minister's will and in terms of the international scene the break might be irreparable. Suez would look small-time, a lovers' tiff. Russell knew this and that others did too, enemies whose interest would be to work for a breach and widen it. He couldn't foretell their actions but their identity was certain. He hadn't a single doubt of it for he'd studied their mind and knew it. Besides, he'd have done the same himself. The rules of the game were the same for all.

Doctor Anthony Shripatrao Deshmukh had been called to Casilda Paine-Pelling. He'd been treating her privately for the two months since her arrival but he didn't know much about her. He knew she'd been recently widowed and in circumstances which she wouldn't discuss. There seemed to be some mystery there or perhaps it was still too close for talk, but she had certainly suffered a serious shock and she was sleeping very badly. He did what he could but was too good a doctor to suppose that he could help much. Time would heal her or maybe wouldn't.

He was an Indian but had never been to India. Nor did he wish to go. What he wanted was money, not a great deal of money since he wasn't avaricious, but enough for the sort of doctoring he desired, a proper surgery, decent tools, the leisure to read and to keep up to date. Ten thousand pounds would do it, even five, and he had as much chance of just five thousand pounds as he had of half a million. So emigrate, go to Australia? His face was brown. To India then? He shuddered. Taxation in India was severer even than in England: it would take him a lifetime to save five thousand. Besides, the idea was alien. So was the country. He'd been born here in England and held a straightforward British passport. No nonsense of Commonwealth citizenship. He was proud of that unreasonably . . . India? He couldn't even speak Hindi. His parents had spoken Marathi, beautiful Brahmin's Marathi, but he'd long since forgotten it. He was as English as the English but his face wasn't white.

So he was condemned to this third-rate practice with two partners he thought barbarians. There weren't many private patients and such as there were were boring, old people with little wrong with them but happy to pay him a guinea or two provided he'd ease their loneliness by chatting to them interminably. He much preferred Casilda Paine-Pelling. To begin with she was intelligent, and there was the hint of some secret as challenge. Her English was almost perfect but he could tell she wasn't English, despite that so English, so county-sounding name. She was Spanish perhaps, or maybe Italian. Latin—he was sure of it.

He sighed as he drove his tatty car. If he could jack up the practice there'd be other Casildas, educated, even stimulating patients. He didn't get those now and never would, Casilda Paine-Pelling was his first new patient in three months. He knew the reputation of the practice—one old doctor in his seventies practising medicine by memory, another much younger but suspect of the bottle. Anthony Shripatrao Deshmukh did the work.

He sighed again as he stopped the car. He needed money for the practice—buy out the old one, squeeze out the young; but he needed it too for other things; he needed it for Bridget, his wife.

His parents had been right, he thought, they'd always opposed the marriage, and not because his wife was white since they were as anglicized as he was. What they'd opposed had been Bridget Macnamee. His father had been a type no longer found, one of the first Indians to join the Indian Civil Service on level terms. Oxford had been heaven to him, the unattainable attained, and life in the I.C.S. another heaven. He'd had a Brahmin's brains and an Englishman's training and he'd gone very near the top indeed. But in twenty-five years' service he'd never doubted where he'd retire to. That hadn't been to a hill station but to the country he sincerely loved.

So it hadn't been a shock to him when his son had brought home a white fiancée; what had shocked the old couple had been Bridget herself. She'd been a nurse in a hospital but neither of them was a social snob; they were much too secure in their own sure position. Nursing was an honourable profession and doctors happily married nurses. Nor was her race an obstacle, though old Sir Ganpatrao's mental picture of the Irish would have sourly amused an Irishman. Not race then, but caste. Caste. For once the doctor's parents had slipped back into Marathi. They were anglicized Indians but had an almost Scottish respect for education. Bridget Macnamee wasn't educated; she was in fact a peasant. This wouldn't do, was indeed a disaster.

As he walked up the outside steps to Casilda's flat Doctor Deshmukh was agreeing with his parents. Bridget had done at first but not for long. He hadn't realized what consumed her or he'd have shied away in simple fright. He wasn't a courageous man. The passionate anti-Englishness, the interminable harping on ancient, decaying, destructive wrongs. A grandfather shot in the Troubles, eh? He'd probably deserved it too—all martyrs were terrible show-offs. And to go on and on about the old fool, the wicked, wicked English, still Cromwell's men. Hundreds of years ago—race memory. Piddle. The extraordinary people who'd started coming to his house. Finally the Great Gesture, appearing suddenly in a sari and scaring him out of his wits. She'd seen it as defiance but he'd seen it as ridiculous. He wasn't a Hindu at that, he was a Christian baptized Anthony.

With ten thousand pounds or even five he could buy off Bridget decently. Then a respectable English housekeeper and he'd bring his widowed father to live with him. The old man had an adequate pension and was comfortable in a home, but the convert Christian Deshmukh was more christian than many born so. The old shouldn't be left to die alone, pastured out in some home however cosy. It was barbarous, uncivilized. And Bridget wouldn't have him but had quietly refused him houseroom ... He was comfortable, wasn't he? He had money to spare, a pension earned dishonourably by exploiting his own people. She'd never said it in words but he'd read the thought and it had broken his last bond to her. He owed her money perhaps, a little money; he owed her nothing else at all.

Casilda Paine-Pelling answered his ring herself. They went through the little hall and into the living-room. He had the easy un-bedside manner of the competent up-to-date doctor and said matter-of-factly:

'I'm sorry you're not feeling well.'

'It's nothing really. I hesitated to call you.' She hadn't a trace of accent.

'That's what I'm for.'

'I do wish I could sleep better.'

'Those pills I gave you——'

'I take a couple as you told me—never more. But they don't seem to bite.'

'Let's have a look at you.'

He examined her, a routine check but thorough and conscientious. 'When did you last get a really good night?'

'I can't remember.'

'Last night?'

'Not good.'

'The night before?'

'Hopeless, I got up in the small hours and went for a walk.'

'Indeed?' He was troubled. He'd heard plenty of stories of sleeplessness and was sceptical as good doctors were, but walking at night was something else. He said, making talk: 'That was the night the aeroplane crashed.'

'I know. I heard the noise of its engines but it seemed a long way off. I didn't catch a glimpse of it but I did see a splash in the bay.'

His face stayed impassive-Indian but his mind was racing furiously. A bomb on the foreshore, a splash in the bay ... But his voice didn't change as he asked her casually: 'A splash in the bay? How did you notice it?'

'I was up on the cliffs.'

'But I thought it was dark as dark could be.'

She smiled. 'If you're thinking I've been seeing things, I've not. It was blowing a gale and pretty dark, but there was a break in the clouds and the moon came through. There was a moon-path on the sea and I saw a splash. Wreckage from the plane, perhaps.'

'It doesn't matter,' he said easily.

... It didn't matter, he'd said, but it mattered like hell. One bomb on the foreshore, a splash in the bay. Wreckage from the plane perhaps. *Or perhaps not wreckage.*

He knew what he must do and how, and his doctor's conscience wasn't troubled. He'd have given her a bigger pill and that would have brought her sleep for perhaps eight hours. Instead he'd give her an injection and that would put her out for at least eighteen. Time to motor up to London, time to be first with a red-hot story.

He turned to his bag but there was something he must know still. She had a boy of three and he might be in the bedroom. One couldn't have the child waking, calling its mother, bawling the house down and bringing in the neighbours. As he bent over his bag he asked:

23

'And how's the boy?'

'He's away. His father's parents have taken him for a week.'

'That'll be nice for them.' He straightened, holding the hypodermic. 'You look pretty tensed up and I'm giving you something to ease it.' He rolled back her sleeve, dabbing the arm with spirit. 'This will really make you sleep, it really will.'

She said almost wistfully: 'I do hope it will. Those pills worked once but the last few days——'

'I guarantee it absolutely.'

He gave her the shot, then settled her on the sofa. 'In ten minutes at most you won't know a thing.'

He shut the door behind him, looking at his watch. It was seven in the evening and a good six hours to London in his beat-up little runabout. That would get him there at one o'clock. One in the morning and London dead. Offices shut but not the one he was going to. People worked all night at newspapers and were very well paid to do so.

They also paid well for a screaming scoop. Not five thousand perhaps, but it wouldn't be chicken feed. Enough at least to start on Bridget.

He began to drive straight to London.

CHAPTER THREE

Martin Dominy found her lying on the sofa and for an instant he thought her dead. But not for long. He'd seen death before and had an instinct for its presence, and he knew enough rough medicine to check her state. He lifted an eyelid and it dropped again easily; he felt her pulse, it was nice and firm. She breathed deeply and easily and when he shook her she sighed. She wasn't dead, she was simply drugged. He went into the bathroom, opening the wall-cupboard . . . Yes, as he'd thought. There were sleeping pills and she'd used them.

He returned to the living-room, sitting down quietly, smoking. He needn't call a doctor, all his training shunned publicity, and though it looked like a modest overdose she wasn't in any danger. She'd had a breakdown when her husband died and kept sleeping pills to cope with it, perfectly respectable sleeping-pills with a formula on the label; she'd had a breakdown and was escaping so he'd wait for her to wake. She might even be glad to see him again.

He watched her as she began to stir. It wouldn't be long now, and he went into the kitchen to put on milk . . . Casilda Paine-Pelling—preposterous, inappropriate name. The overtones were upper crust, some manor in the Shires with hunting noises off. Martin grinned. Casilda was pure Spanish, had in fact been a servant in just such a house. Tom Pelling had wanted to marry her and Charles Russell had approved the match. He had an eye for a vigorous woman and an instinct for a nice one, and his staff didn't marry freely by presenting some well-connected deb. It wasn't one of his illusions that an agent should stay a bachelor—let him marry and good luck to him—but the choice could be important since the wrong one could be fatal. Casilda had passed with Charles Russell at once. He'd seen in her two virtues which he valued more than much fine gold, a fierce Catalan independence and unshakable loyalty. She'd been a servant—what of it? Thomas Paine-Pelling had expected certain difficulties, but Russell had made none at all and had gone to the wedding happily.

Poor Thomas Paine-Pelling who had bought it rather squalidly. The assignment hadn't been one which Russell liked, but he was used to odd assignments and it had been difficult to refuse. There'd been a Commonwealth state in Africa which had been eating a lot of money, British taxpayers' money since they hadn't had the option. Russell thought these payments Danegeld but there were politicians who thought otherwise. Still, there were limits and this stateling had overstepped them. There was four million pounds' worth of machinery rusting on a quayside. That had happened before and the Ministry concerned had sighed, but inefficiency was one thing, open corruption a little different. The Minister wasn't squeamish but a newspaper was gunning for him. It had some of the story too, and it wasn't cold. Four million pounds' worth of expensive modern equipment was to be sold to a Greek scrap dealer. Sold for the personal account of the man they called Father Toby.

Russell had been asked to take a look. It had to be done discreetly since face in these matters was paramount, but if it could be discovered without wounding notoriously tender sensibilities . . .

He had sent out Tom Pelling and he hadn't come back. He'd been found dead in bed in the best hotel and the manner of his killing had not been African. He hadn't been mutilated, simply shot in cold blood and sleeping. Charles Russell had reacted in a wholly personal fury, something which as an

26

official he seldom allowed himself and as a good one he never indulged. He didn't indulge it now though he knew he could. He could guess to three men who had murdered Tom Pelling and all of them were members of Father Toby's personal bodyguard. All of them were communists, as was Tobias himself in all but name. They were very well paid but they weren't immortal. No indeed, these hired Czechs were not immortal.

Charles Russell had ground his teeth but held his hand. He was a good official first and the risk too great. There was something called the Commonwealth, meaningless in terms of power but explicably important to the Office which bore its name. Discipline had won at last but the personal price had been heavy.

Casilda had been shattered and Martin still shared her sorrow. He'd liked and respected Pelling and he'd seen that his wife adored him. There was a boy of three too, the reason for her presence here. The Security Executive was generous to its widows and she could have returned to her Catalan home and lived almost grandly. But she would have thought it defeat to do so. Her husband had been English—so was his son. She'd bring him up English, it was an obligation and inescapable, so she'd taken a flat in Burke Hoe for the worst of her grief. It was really the end of nowhere but nowhere was where she wanted, and after three months she'd think again, she'd plan. Charles Russell would help her, she liked Charles Russell. He wrote regularly and sometimes rang. Once he'd even come down himself.

This time he'd sent Martin Dominy, who was watching Casilda stirring. He went to look at the milk again and when he returned her eyes were open.

'Remember me?'

'Of course. Tom's friend.' Her voice was weak but it wasn't shaky. Martin, relieved, said comfortably:

27

'Had a good sleep?'

'A beauty.' She looked around. 'What time is it?'

'Three o'clock.'

'Three o'clock!' She stared. 'What day?'

'It's Friday of course.'

She said something in Spanish he didn't catch.

'What day did you think?' He rubbed his chin, deciding on candour. She was a woman you could be candid with. 'I went into the bathroom and saw the pills. You must have taken quite a few.'

'I didn't take any.'

He didn't answer, fetching the milk; he knew she wasn't lying, she didn't lie; he gave her the milk and she thanked him with a smile. He liked it that she didn't fuss. She asked at length:

'What are you doing here?'

'I'd a job in Burke Hoe so I naturally looked you up.'

'How did you get in?'

'I picked the lock.'

'But why? I might have been out.'

He spread his hands. 'I feel things . . . Sometimes . . . '

She didn't waste time in comment but finished the milk. 'The last thing I remember was about seven o'clock last night. And I really haven't taken a single pill.'

'You'd better tell me,' he said.

'I sleep badly as you've gathered and it's been getting a good deal worse. The doctor gave me the pills you found but for several days they haven't worked. So I asked him to come last night and he gave me a shot.'

'Quite a shot—twenty hours.'

'I suppose it was but he's a very good doctor. He's an Indian but a nice one.'

Martin said: 'An Indian?'

'A very English Indian. He's never been to India.'

'Still . . . ' He considered it professionally. 'I told you I'd come to Burke Hoe on a job. Have you been reading the papers of late?'

'Not very much but I've heard the news. A bomb dropped on the beach but it didn't go off.'

'Did your Indian doctor mention that?'

'No . . . Well, in a way. Not the bomb itself, though.'

'Well?'

'I told him I'd been sleeping worse than ever. He asked for details so I said I'd slept badly the night before, and the night before that was terrible. I'd got up in the middle of it and gone for a walk on the cliffs.'

'That was all?'

'No, not quite. I told him I'd heard an aircraft a long way off. I didn't even see it but I did see something else. The moon had come through and I saw a splash in the bay.'

'A splash in the bay?' Martin Dominy repeated.

'That's right.'

'You've told nobody else?'

'No—why should I?' She smiled a little wryly. 'I've got precious few people to talk to. I wouldn't have told the doctor if it hadn't come up quite naturally.'

'*Then you're not to repeat it to a living soul.*'

'I'll do just as you say.' She took his vehemence almost casually, almost as an order. She knew he was in the Executive, a colleague of Tom's and a friend at that. He looked at her with respect. She'd been sleeping for twenty hours and she wasn't beautiful. She had the heavy robust shoulders of a woman who had worked with them; she wasn't tall. But her hands were long and sensitive, her forehead serene, her eyebrows were strong black bows. She was clearly a woman of character which it mightn't be wise to probe too deep. Instead he said simply:

'I'd better explain.'

29

'Tom taught me never to ask,' she said.

'I know, but I'm going to tell you. I'm here on a job and the job was that bomb. Not the bomb itself, but the background, the story. It was dropped by the Americans and in Spain they dropped two. Remember?' She nodded. 'Here they only dropped one, we've accepted that so far, but there are people it would suit if they'd dropped a second. One they couldn't recover. Out in the bay.'

She nodded again at once. 'There are people who'd like to make play with that.' She was quick, he was thinking, and something more. She added almost inaudibly: 'I've guessed it was they killed Tom.'

He let it pass without comment since he didn't have a useful one. 'So you saw a splash in the bay—'

'I'm sure of it.'

'And mentioned it to this Indian?'

'Yes.'

'Who promptly knocks you out for a night and a day.'

'I see,' she said slowly. 'I think I see.'

'Could you ring up his surgery?'

'Of course.' She did so, finally turning. 'He hasn't been at the surgery all day.'

'His house? Do you know his wife?'

'He brought her here to tea once but we didn't hit it off. She's white but she isn't English. Frankly, I didn't take to her.'

'You quarrelled?' he asked.

She looked at him pityingly. 'I'm Spanish. I hide my feelings.'

'You're rather a frightening woman.' It wasn't the adjective he'd have chosen at leisure but she passed it with indifference. She didn't seem greatly interested in what other people thought of her. He asked again: 'Could you ring her house?'

'If you wish it,' she said politely.

She turned again minutes later, the oval face still expressionless. 'Doctor Deshmukh didn't go home last night but he did tell his wife he was coming here.' She passed him the telephone courteously. The gesture was a simple one, the manner high hidalgo. The battered, ancient telephone could have been gold or myrrh or frankincense. 'You'll want to telephone to London.'

'Thanks.'

He rang to the Executive and shortly was on to Charles Russell himself. Russell listened to him carefully; he considered and then decided. 'Is there any further danger to the lady you were mentioning?'

'On what I know I'd say there wasn't.'

'I'll send a man down to make sure there isn't. Meanwhile return to London at once. Report to me personally.'

There was an axiom in the Security Executive, one which Lord Normer would have approved of as a scientist. It was that the best working hypothesis was the simplest which covered the known facts, and Martin Dominy had adopted it unhesitatingly. He was talking next morning in Russell's comfortably informal office and Charles Russell was listening, not interrupting. Casilda Paine-Pelling had seen something drop into the bay at night and had mentioned it to her doctor. Who was the husband of a card-carrying party member. The doctor had promptly put Casilda out and had disappeared as promptly; he'd gone neither to his practice nor his home; he had information and meant to use it, and with his wife's known connections that use would be political. He was probably in London now and he'd know where to take his story.

Charles Russell had listened quietly, nodding. It had struck him as sound deduction, indeed he would have been mildly mistrustful if a working operator had come up with a theory more complicated. Martin Dominy was a working operator but one day might be rather more. He was well worth

sophisticating and Charles Russell began to do so. 'Quite,'
he said finally. 'Perfectly logical and it covers the facts as you
know them.' He was conscious this might sound pompous and
pomposity he detested; he smiled and added blandly: 'Do
you mind if I play at schoolmasters?'

'I know I've a great deal to learn, sir.'

The tone had been mild but Martin had moved up one;
he could hit back gracefully and that was important. Russell
said imperturbably: 'I don't think I quite deserved that, but
let's start at the beginning. So Casilda gives this doctor
information which admittedly could be awkward if it got
into certain hands. That's common ground and I don't dispute
it. He then gives her an injection which he must have known
would keep her quiet for a good few hours.' Charles Russell
looked at Dominy. 'Now why should he do that?'

'To give himself time.'

'But why did he want it? If he were going to whom you
assumed the story would keep while he motored to London,
or he could have told his wife and left her to pass it on.'

Martin didn't answer since he didn't have a good one.

'Don't think that I'm trying to be clever, pulling a reasonable
theory apart for the pleasure of seeing it crumble. The plain
fact is that sitting here I've the advantage of you. I've a machine
which you hadn't and I've been using it discreetly. You rang
me yesterday at half-past three and I used the rest of that
day and some of the night in making some simple inquiries.
Would you care to hear the results of them?'

'Very much indeed, sir.'

'Then this Doctor Deshmukh's wife is what you already
know she is, a card-carrying party member. Which gives her
potential for mischief but not, until we confirm it, the training
or the ability to indulge in mischief actively. And so far we
haven't confirmed it. Naturally you never know, and you
can take it that our Irish friends have started digging on

32

Mrs Deshmukh's past. I'd like very much more on her folder before writing her off as harmless. That will take time but I've plenty on Deshmukh himself meanwhile.' Charles Russell smiled. 'In a place like Burke Hoe you can't hide a pin. The local police know everything and they've really been very helpful.'

'Deshmukh is known to the local police?'

'Not in the newspaper sense at all, but in a godforsaken hole like that everyone knows everyone else's business. And Deshmukh's is pretty dim.'

'Dim?'

'Shaky. Unhappy too. He's rather a good doctor in rather a terrible practice. That's happened to Indians before, even when they're as anglicized as he is. He's married this party member too, and it's pretty well known it hasn't worked. Now what does that suggest to you?'

'That I'm glad I'm not Doctor Deshmukh.'

'And if you were?'

'I'd try to break out.'

'With what?'

Martin said slowly: 'Money.'

'Good—we advance. So you're an unhappy country doctor in a third-class little watering place. The Americans drop a bomb on it and once before in Spain they slipped a couple. They've been very quick on the trigger in denying that happened here, but a patient tells you she heard their aircraft. She saw a splash in the bay as well——'

'It's a story,' Martin Dominy said.

'And it might sound like a scoop if you could get there with it first. But you must be sure of being first: in Fleet Street that's what they'd pay you for. So you knock her out for a good long time, drive to London, to a newspaper——'

'Which one?' Martin asked.

'Which one would you choose yourself?'

33

'The one with the biggest circulation. The one which would pay most.'

'The *Gong?*'

'Yes, I think so.'

'So did the doctor. Besides, I've found out he reads the thing.'

'You're sure?' Martin asked.

'Quite sure. I've been cheating again since I rang the editor. He belongs to my club and he's held in high esteem there. So I rang him and I taped it.' Charles Russell looked innocent. 'That's an occupational risk when you talk to the Executive. Care to hear it?'

'Of course.'

A secretary brought in the recorder and Russell threw the switch. There was a whirr, then his own clear voice:

'Good morning, Henry.'

'Good morning, Charles. What can I do for the Security Executive?'

'Information as usual, the sort we don't have.'

'I'll try.'

What have you got on that affair at Burke Hoe?'

'Nothing. I wish I had.'

'Anybody offered it?'

There was a disillusioned chuckle. 'Ah, so you know something. I thought it must be that since it wasn't to ask me to lunch. So I might as well confirm what you appear to know already. An Indian came in last night and wanted money. What he was trying to sell was a report that a second bomb had been dropped into the bay.'

'May I ask what you did with it?'

'The story? There wasn't one.' The voice became gently offended. 'Dammit Charles, you know the *Gong*. It's not the intellectuals' favourite son but it does happen to be a newspaper. A *news*paper. What sort of story was that? Somebody sees a splash in the sea, not even the man who brings the report of it. It could have been a piece of a breaking-up aircraft— anything. In the circumstances, which we needn't discuss, it would be front-page news or nothing at all, and to the night editor it was nothing. He was quite right too. Print that and you'd need a follow-up. And where do you get that? How *could* you get a follow-up?'

'You threw this Indian out then?'

'I told you—we're a newspaper. Hundreds of amateur newshounds try to sell us a load of rubbish.'

'Would this one try elsewhere, d'you think?'

'I dare say he might. It might be worth an inch at most, but no self-respecting newspaper would run it as a story.'

'Not even the *Custodian?*'

'But that isn't a newspaper.' The voice was openly contemptuous now. 'It's a journal of opinion, holy writ to all the softies. Have you seen it this morning? No? You're a sensible man. It was raving against the Americans, positively rabid. Terrible old hat, at that. No wonder nobody reads it.'

'So one couldn't have sold this story to what you properly call a newspaper?'

'There isn't a story to sell, my friend.'

'Well, thank you, Henry.'

'I hope I've helped.'

Russell switched the tape off, returning to Martin Dominy. Martin said quietly:

'I'm sorry I got it wrong, sir.'

'You didn't get it wrong and I didn't say so. You had a sensible hypothesis but I had more facts. And what do you think happens now?'

'I suppose we've picked up this doctor's trail?'

'We have. The third paper he tried. He'll be getting a bit discouraged by now.'

'And what do we do, sir?'

35

'Nothing. He's breaking no law and this isn't a police state.'

'Suppose he goes home and tells his wife.'

'It's still not a story, though I'll admit that I'd rather he didn't. It's still not a story but it could put ideas into people's heads. The wrong sort of people.'

'Starting something?'

'*Sparking* it. Maybe.'

'More serious than the *Custodian*'s squeals?'

Russell said: 'Much more serious.'

'But I wish we could take some action, sir.'

'We can't. We'll have to wait.' Charles Russell smiled urbanely. 'Waiting,' he said, 'is something you'll have to get good at.'

CHAPTER FOUR

Anthony Shripatrao Deshmukh was exhausted. He'd been trudging from one newspaper to another and that had tired him physically, and the bitter disappointment had left him spent. He hadn't thought it out deeply but his hopes had soared sky-high; he knew nothing of newspapers except that he'd heard they paid well, and he'd stumbled on a story which any newspaper would give money for. Or so he had thought. He'd have to be first with the news no doubt, but he'd reacted fast enough to that. Mrs Paine-Pelling wouldn't talk for some time. She couldn't. He had a scoop and that was valuable.

Now it seemed that it wasn't, he'd got it quite wrong. He'd been to five newspapers and four hadn't been interested. The fifth had been at least polite and a man had explained to him coolly. This wasn't a story but was just possibly a line on one. The man at the desk would speak to a superior and it wasn't inconceivable that they'd send somebody down to Burke Hoe, somebody of their own to investigate a report that something—anything—had fallen from the skies besides a bomb. As likely as not there was nothing in it, but if there was something usable they'd remember Anthony Deshmukh. The man at the desk had made a note of his name and address. A fiver perhaps or even a tenner, but that wasn't an undertaking. Doctor Deshmukh had sighed. Ten pounds wouldn't help him to modernize the practice, it wouldn't even help him to get rid of Bridget Deshmukh. He hadn't telephoned to warn her of his absence. They hadn't that sort of relationship now, had indeed hardly spoken since she'd declined to house his father.

Anthony Deshmukh hadn't eaten all day and was suddenly very hungry. He looked at his watch—it was half-past two; he collected his car from the garage where he had left it, paying the outrageous bill reluctantly, on an impulse driving to Old Street. There was an Indian restaurant in Old Street, one remembered from his student days, and he hadn't eaten Indian for several years. He parked the old car in Bunhill Row; he ate and returned to it.

It wouldn't start.

He opened the bonnet unhopefully for he was no sort of mechanic and knew it. He checked the oil: there was oil all right. Petrol? There seemed to be petrol too. He went back into the driving seat, pressing the starter and pumping the choke. A depressing, protesting noise. Not a kick.

The attendant came over to him. 'Can't you start her, guv?'

'I'm afraid I can't.'

The attendant looked in the still-open bonnet, producing a plastic-handled screwdriver which he held across a plug. 'Just try her again.'

Deshmukh pressed the self-starter.

'No spark.'

Doctor Deshmukh climbed down again, standing helplessly by the attendant. The attendant took off the distributor head, wiping the contacts, then peering at the points, flicking them against the spring. 'That seems to be all right,' he said.

'You're a mechanic?'

'Christ, no.' The other laughed. 'But I've got an old car.' He added without malice: 'Even older than this one.'

Deshmukh was silent for he had realized he was a foreigner. He didn't often feel one but now he did. He spoke beautiful English, much better than the attendant's, but the attendant knew something of motor cars. He wasn't a mechanic but to

Deshmukh he seemed Olympian; he asked him respectfully:

'Can you tell me what's gone wrong?'

The attendant shrugged. 'Might be anything electrical, a short circuit or the coil gone.'

To Shripatrao Deshmukh he was talking double-Dutch. Sir Ganpatrao had had a car but naturally a driver too. The doctor didn't have a driver but he hoped one day to have one. Cars were very much things not people, not work for a twice-born doctor.

'But I've got to get home.'

'You won't in that. I'd get a taxi in the City Road——'

'I live in North Devon, I've got to get home.'

He had, he thought—he really had. He could cook up some lie for Bridget, perhaps that his father had sent for him unexpectedly. She wouldn't approve though she'd probably believe it, but he'd left his partners without a warning and he had a surgery next morning. They wouldn't take it matily if he left them to take his duty. He despised them as medical savages but they were very strict on timekeeping. It would be two of them to one of him and he happened to be an Indian. He said suddenly, shrilly: 'What shall I do, please? *Please.*'

He was hating himself but helpless. The beautiful English had gone with the wind, the voice from his chest into the clipped chatter of the Eurasian. And he wasn't a Eurasian, he was Anthony Deshmukh, a doctor and a good one. He clutched at that but in a crisis it was irrelevant. He said again: 'What shall I do? Please help.' He was utterly humiliated for the truth had stood up and mocked him. He was half a jump from panic and for no reason in the world at all.

The attendant said placidly: 'You won't get home in that tonight.'

'What shall I do? I've *got* to get back.'

'Then leave her here and go home by train.' The attendant

looked at Deshmukh curiously. He seemed to be in a frightful flap. Of course he was a wog and wogs got excited easily. Just the same it was embarrassing. But he was a kindly man and said amiably enough: 'Look guv, this isn't the end of the world. It's happened before and we've worked out a sort of drill for it.' He felt in a pocket and produced a dirty card. 'That's a garage we use when cars break down here. I'll give them a ring and they'll come and fetch her. You give me your address and I'll give them that as well. Your telephone number too and they'll ring you and quote the damage. Then you fetch her when she's ready. Right?'

'Right,' Deshmukh said. His voice had gone down to his chest again but he was more humiliated than ever. It had been absurdly simple, absurdly smooth. An attendant in a car park, talking some London dialect . . .

Deshmukh gave him a pound for he wasn't mean and the gesture of tipping was in a real sense restorative. There was an afternoon train from Waterloo and he had plenty of time to catch it. He knew this part of London well, and began to walk down to the Bank and the Underground station. There was a line which went direct to Waterloo, serving the south-western suburbs and in the rush hour a penance. They called it the Drain but it wasn't yet the rush hour.

He passed a telephone booth without a pang. He ought to ring Bridget but he wasn't on ringing terms with her.

He bought a ticket from the coin-machine, going down to the train on the travolator. He didn't walk but let it carry him, for there were plenty of trains and he wasn't pressed for time. He was feeling a little better now, glad that he'd given that man a pound. He couldn't afford it, he'd considered ten shillings, but now he was happy he'd made it a pound.

There was a train on the right-hand platform ready to move, and he made the first doors as they started to close. But at once he wished he hadn't. It wasn't the rush hour but the compartment was fairly full. Of other Indians. If you called them that. Deshmukh didn't.

. . . East Bengalis—he detested them. He was genuinely indifferent to their most peculiar form of Islam and secretly rather happy that today they weren't technically Indians, but he was an Indian Christian of Brahmin blood and East Bengalis outraged both inheritances. Gang rape, he was thinking, and thuggee—the lot. He couldn't understand a word they said. How they chattered, like monkeys, pawing each other and giggling like girls. The English Anthony Deshmukh was disapproving in an English way and the Brahmin Shripatrao Deshmukh was intolerably affronted. Why, they weren't even clean. He supposed he could just about stand them for the five or six minutes the journey took.

The train rattled on, then slowed unexpectedly, stopped. For a moment nothing happened, then a sudden and almost blinding flash. All the lights went out together and the carriage began to fill with smoke.

Anthony Deshmukh sat very still.

In the compartment behind him the guard wasn't worried. He had his telephone out and had connected it to the pinch wires. He knew what had happened for he'd had it once before. A pick-up shoe had broken, scraped, and the arc had welded it solid to the conductor rail. The fuses had properly blown and that was that. The guard was annoyed but in no way scared. It would take some time to free the shoe, then they'd have to send something to tow them out. Single-line working in the worst of the rush hour, chaos but he'd be out of it. Some overtime too. He made his report in a calm bored voice.

In Doctor Deshmukh's carriage it was neither calm nor bored. There was an instant of silence, then a babel in Bengali. The voices were high and shrill, they always were. Now they were febrile. Just like his own, Doctor Anthony thought—

41

his own half an hour ago. He set his teeth for he'd just learnt a lesson.

The smoke was increasing steadily.

Somebody had a torch out, flashing it round. In the swirling smoke it wasn't effective, but it showed the taut faces, insensate primeval fear. In a moment they'd break, do anything.

Doctor Anthony Deshmukh prayed.

It came as the prayer faded, a sudden rush. They were at the doors, all of them, clawing and fighting, gone.

. . . Ridiculous, contemptible. The English looked into motorcars; they told you what was wrong with them and they told you how to handle it. Absurd to imagine danger on a line which carried millions.

The smoke seemed to be getting thicker and they'd be under the River Thames by now. They could drown perhaps if they didn't burn.

He thought of both deaths: they were equally terrifying.

The torch was still surviving and one of them had a knife out. He was trying to force the doors. He hadn't moved them an inch but he'd cut the rubber sealing. The smoke poured in thicker, they were fighting insanely. Perhaps two dozen of them—animals. Three were already down, obscenely trampled. It was Anthony Deshmukh's idea of hell.

He groaned but he rose. Then he was at the doors and pulling feebly. He felt the knife in his lower ribs. For a last instant a doctor, he thought like a doctor.

The brute knew where to put it.

He fell at last slowly and at once was underfoot.

CHAPTER FIVE

Anthony Deshmukh's death had annoyed Charles Russell. He liked cause and effect, a world where he could observe the first, then safely foretell the second, and Deshmukh's death had been wholly unnecessary, outside any cause he could see or guess, irrelevant to the developments he increasingly feared. It was therefore untidy and he detested untidiness.

But there was pity in his emotions too. Poor little basket, he'd had it rough, a squalid and unseemly death which he hadn't deserved and hadn't sought. Russell wasn't a blind admirer of all things Indian. He'd served in India and hadn't enjoyed it, but he'd escaped the insensitive arrogance of the standard old India hand. Indians could exacerbate as no other people on earth could—the bland assumption of an unquestioned moral superiority, the staggering inefficiency in petty things. But they were seldom cruel when nowadays that was exceptional, and sometimes they could try though not for long. Fragile was the word for them. It was all quite hopeless and always would be. The pervading stench of excrement which somehow you got used to, the more frightening stink of sheer bad luck which they never contrived to wash away. You couldn't really do anything for them but send them a little food. But not too much. In the end one couldn't help them. They'd collapse quite inevitably, four hundred million anachronisms, and no one so anachronistic as the westernized, anglicized Indian.

Poor little basket, he'd certainly bought it. An intelligent doctor in a struggling, wretched practice. Picks a white wife and picks her wrong. Bridget Macnamee. Russell had her papers out and was reading them a second time. The file was a little thicker now, his distaste for it acuter. An Anglo-Irishman himself, he was the last man to be deluded by the stage-Irish name, but a tiny fringe of Irishman still cherished ancestral grudges in a way he considered stage-Irish. Secret drillings in the mountains, foolish bombings in the bogs. Ninety-nine of a hundred Irishmen were happily contemporary, or as happily as that allowed, making a little money at last, freezing out hopeful Germans who had seen a cheap investment in Irish land and lived to regret it bitterly. To a twentieth-century Irishman the schoolroom antics of Bridget's friends were as embarrassing as an over-zealous Zionism was a bore to the modern Israeli. And they had even less effect on ordinary lives.

Still, it was there on paper now, ludicrous, faintly shaming. A grandfather killed in the Troubles and (she'd resent this more) an elder brother lawfully tried by his own Government and sentenced to imprisonment for some pointless but armed stupidity on the Border. She'd repudiate that Government, calling it a half-alien sham. Even that didn't make her dangerous; she wasn't the type to pop bombs in British letterboxes. But it did make her vulnerable. There was more than one English body which would be delighted to recruit her, herself and the crumbling hatreds which only defeated men could love. More than one organization would be very pleased to have her.

And the most formidable of them had done so.

Charles Russell shrugged. He supposed he should feel angry and decidedly he was irritated, but he was also a fellow-countryman and not without understanding. He felt something like admiration too. The woman was obsessed, a bore, but she wasn't for that contemptible.

In any case he wouldn't credit that she was dangerous, not

on this negative background of simple silliness. Something else might come in, something positive, a connection. He would credit that when he saw it but he wasn't impressed by this whipped-up wind. She was a party member now no doubt, but Russell well knew what that meant. People who carried cards were seldom agents. True. But they'd know where to go with a political titbit, and a splash in the bay was at any rate interesting.

He considered it carefully. Doctor Deshmukh might have told his wife but events as Russell knew them suggested strongly that he hadn't. He'd drugged Casilda Paine-Pelling, driving straightaway to London. Now he was dead. No doubt he could have telephoned but there hadn't been motive to do so. Rather markedly to the contrary. Casilda had seen the incident but Dominy had silenced her. Several newspapers knew of it too by now but they wouldn't run it seriously. So the dottier weekend journals might go raving on interminably but they'd rave about dropping a single bomb, the orthodox anti-Americanism which Russell and his peers despised. And so did many others though for a rather different reason. They were simply bored stiff with it.

Nevertheless there'd been a splash in the bay and that was worth thought if nothing else. Charles Russell gave it deliberate thought. A second bomb? Extremely improbable. Casilda Paine-Pelling had seen a splash and she hadn't had binoculars. That meant a couple of miles at most, and for two miles off-shore it wasn't deep. If another bomb had dropped there it would have been simple to recover it and a wholly senseless risk to deny its existence. They'd recovered a second in Spain with much more toil. So accepting the story, then what had it been? The *Gong*'s editor had speculated: a piece of a breaking-up aircraft—anything.

Anything might alas be right. In the sea perhaps but as likely elsewhere since it wasn't the splash in the sea which was worrying Russell. An aircraft had broken up which had carried a bomb. Nuclear bombs were uncomfortably complex, part of weapon systems more so . . .

Charles Russell didn't speculate but wrote it down instead:

1. *The aircraft left Germany hastily and it wasn't a type which normally carries bombs.*
2. *It broke up in a storm where it shouldn't have been and it dropped its bomb doing so.*
3. *I suspect there's much more to a nuclear bomb than a casing with hell inside it.*

Russell underlined 3 thoughtfully. It was high time he talked to Lord Normer again.

4. *One of the crew is still alive. Dominy tells me he tried to check on him but was told he was still unconscious. It was an American doctor who told him so since they've flown one in to look after him.*

He picked up the telephone, telling Martin Dominy to return to Burke Hoe since if anything broke it would be there that it did so. Russell was hoping that he didn't sound mysterious, something he disliked as unprofessional. Martin's commission was still unlimited but Russell had two suggestions. It would be wise to keep contact with Casilda Paine-Pelling and even more helpful if he could talk to the survivor. If he could now get near him. To report, of course.

Good hunting.

Martin Dominy took the first of these suggestions first, calling on Casilda after he'd telephoned her from London. He had told her of Deshmukh's death before the local newspapers or perhaps some gabby neighbour could bring her the news and guessing with it. Avoidable guessing was always to be avoided. She made him tea with a slice of lemon and he watched her long hands with pleasure. He'd been told to keep contact but not for what purpose, and he hadn't expected that she would receive him with news of her own. But she said across her tea cup:

'Bridget Deshmukh came to see me just after you telephoned.'

He was surprised and she noticed it, explaining at once. 'I thought it odd at the time myself, but now I suppose it was natural. I told you he'd brought her here once before, and though we got on rather badly I was the last person in Burke Hoe to see her husband alive. She knew that he'd called here, but I've told you that before.'

'You received her with pleasure?' He could guess that she had not.

'Not with pleasure but with lemon tea. She asked for milk.' Casilda smiled. 'What else would you have me do—bawl her out like a fisherwoman?' By now she was almost bilingual but occasionally made a tiny slip. 'Besides, she's a woman and now she's a widow. So we've one thing in common if nothing else.'

'That I can see.'

He told her the sorry story, Deshmukh's visit to London, all of it. When she'd married Tom Pelling Charles Russell had approved of her and he'd been told to keep contact, which hadn't been done for nothing. Russell hadn't been explicit for he'd had nothing to be explicit with. But no doubt he'd been doing some thinking and so had Martin Dominy. Casilda could be important if . . .

If what? He didn't know that but nor did Russell.

But she was talking again in her quick strong voice. 'So Deshmukh put me to sleep to give himself time. Time to get in with the story first.'

He was impressed that she didn't sound angry but was

47

taking it almost casually. The action had been an outrage but it hadn't been, well, an insult. Her body had been misused but not herself, not the essential Casilda. He managed to suppress a smile. Her name was now Paine-Pelling and it could hardly be more misleading. She asked again:

'So he knocked me out to give himself time?'

'So it seems.'

She dismissed the matter finally. 'That's over and done with but the rest of it isn't—what I saw that night I was walking. Bridget could hear of that or find it out.'

He considered it with care, a valid point. 'Deshmukh went straight to London and I don't think he'll have rung her back. If she had she wouldn't have come to you for news.'

She nodded, accepting it. 'But won't there have to be an inquest on Doctor Deshmukh? And won't it all come out there?'

'I hardly think so—why should it? The coroner will be inquiring how Deshmukh got knifed, then was trampled to death with the others in a panic. I doubt if he'll have much time for why Deshmukh came to London, far less for how he spent his morning. Not that you're not right in theory. His wife *could* discover it.' Martin leant forward, making his point in turn. 'Assuming, that is, that she had reason to try to. But they weren't on good terms and she'll probably think he went to London to see some woman, or maybe to fish for another job. She hasn't a line that anything else exists.'

'But mightn't it be awkward if she stumbled on it later?'

'It'd still be worthless news-wise. It's an un-story.'

'An un-story to whom?' She thought, then added quietly: 'I know Bridget is a communist.'

'And how did you know that?'

'I didn't know but now I do—I found out when she came to see me. When she found I'd got nothing to tell her she started to talk herself. She has almost no friends here and she'd just lost a husband. I could feel sorry for her if I didn't hate everything she stands for. Anyway, she began to talk and that sort of chatter gives everything away. The words she used, the double-talk. It wasn't my fault that her husband was dead but it was something she called the system's.'

He didn't answer her directly for he was trying not to smile again. He could see the scene clearly, the black eyebrows arching, the long hands still, the cool Catalan refusal to be drawn into pointless natter. She'd have let Bridget talk, she'd have let her discharge emotion, but she wouldn't have been involved in it, not a single hair of her well-brushed head.

'So she read you a lecture on communism?'

'No, not exactly. She's a communist all right but she knows nothing of genuine marxism. I know more myself, I could have tripped her up easily. We've the same sort in Spain and they're no more communists than you are.' She waited, then went on coolly. 'What Bridget wants is to square her bill.'

'For what?' he asked. 'For some social injustice?'

She made a contemptuous face. 'That's words. How do you say it—abstractions, yes? But it isn't ideas which drive Bridget Deshmukh. It will be something in the past, I think. The long-dead past. She's Irish, pig-Irish.'

'You're observant and pretty shrewd, you know.'

'Not shrewd—I'm a woman. So is she and I don't like her. I suppose I should. She isn't wicked and she's got guts. But there it is.'

He didn't answer again, thinking how unusual it was for a woman to admit she disliked another. You were usually left to find out for yourself and the process could be extravagant both in time and in embarrassment. Casilda Paine-Pelling was rather wasted in Burke Hoe.

He looked at her uncertainly. Come to that she was simply wasted.

'Bridget's only a party member,' he said.

'That wouldn't stop her being dangerous. If she got hold of that story——'

'I told you I don't think she'll do that now.'

'Or another,' she said.

He looked up from his cup, surprised for the second time. 'Another story? What do you mean?'

She shrugged and he didn't press her. She liked him for that. He was a type she could get along with, the intelligent man with a native mistrust of pure intelligence. She'd been married to an Englishman, had borne him a son and now mourned him in loneliness; she'd learnt much about Englishmen and had some simple effective tests for them. One of them was what games they played. Rugby football, for instance—ugh! The mud, the awful matiness, the warm beers afterwards. Mother Mary in heaven what a travesty of a game, though one mustn't be too severe on them since presumably they were too impoverished to afford a proper ball. But Tom had played the other game, the one her own world played. So had Martin Dominy and it made him more acceptable. She knew because he had told her, for he'd come to their home quite often. She'd been at ease with him then, was at ease with him now, or as much at ease as the widow of a murdered man could feel. A widow of a murdered man, and Spanish.

She might tolerate him, Martin thought, but he'd the impression that he'd lost face with her; he'd been her husband's friend and he worked for the Executive. Which was still one life down in the score of blood and that lost life her husband's. He watched her sit impassively, unhappy, still unavenged, and in a way he mustn't think about a formidably dangerous woman. Of course this wasn't Spain—she'd know that consciously—but Spanish she'd been born and that she'd die. She wouldn't make open demands on him but her mind was a

Latin's and would work in a Latin way. There were people who'd find that funny. Martin didn't.

He said on an impulse: 'There's an American alive still in the hospital. Russell told me to go and see him. If I can get near him.'

She was interested at once, the sad face alert again. He felt a momentary pang, for it had been a mention of Charles Russell's name which had sparked her into sudden life. She was the last woman in the world he would ever think of falling for, indeed he was rather scared of her, but he'd been sitting drinking tea with her and she'd been courteous, pleased to see him; but he'd mentioned Charles Russell and promptly she was alive again; she was saying with new-found emphasis:

'Russell sent you to the hospital?'

'He did.'

'Where Bridget is still a nurse. A communist.'

'And where an American from that aircraft is still alive.'

'You went there before and they told you he was unconscious.' She didn't seem greatly interested in an injured American airman but added with a hint of bite: 'Did you believe them?'

'I didn't disbelieve them. I hadn't a reason to do so.'

She said again stubbornly: 'Bridget Deshmukh is a nurse in the Farracombe hospital.'

This time he nodded.

'It's a very small hospital.'

'Where I'm going again this evening.' He finished his tea and rose, asking her as she held the door: 'May I call on you again?'

She said astonishingly clearly: 'You may since this is England but in my country you wouldn't yet wish to.'

In the little hospital at Farracombe Lieutenant Walter Johnson stirred, opening his eyes on a world he hadn't expected to see again. He could remember that he'd jumped for it and

51

that his parachute had opened, but he hadn't known where he was nor been able to see. As he'd come down the air had got rougher, sudden eddies and gusts which rocked him helplessly. He knew what they meant for he'd jumped before. It could blow half a gale in the open sky and you wouldn't feel a thing of it but once you began to swing like this you were dangerously near the unseen ground. It might be woods or it might be hills. Hills meant valleys and savage side draughts. Hills—no one there. He'd stared down into the darkness but seen nothing. He hadn't been ready, he'd been taut, unrelaxed. He'd been right about the valley though, since he'd smashed into the rock face first.

And after that nothing.

Now he looked round the small room, savouring it. It was a hospital, he decided, by his own standards a little primitive, but it was clean and there was a nurse. She was sitting on a chair and quietly knitting.

He tried to move and found he couldn't. For an instant panic took him and he called to her weakly: 'Nurse.'

She looked up at once, coming over to the bed. He asked the conditioned question: 'Nurse, what happened?'

'You jumped on your parachute and you landed very badly.' She smiled, adding the professional, the meaningless reassurance. 'You're quite all right.'

'Where am I?'

'In England. A place called Farracombe.'

An appalling thought struck him, as cruel as the crash. 'My bag,' he said.

'What bag was that?' Now that he was conscious at last her first duty was calling the doctor, but she was a competent nurse and her patient was exciting himself. She didn't want that and nor would the doctor. She said soothingly: 'I'll have to get the doctor now. He'll know about your things. We took them when they brought you in.'

He tried to move an arm and failed, then somehow moved the other. He grabbed at the nurse's hand. She had a country-woman's face, a little stupid, and a motherly-looking bosom. He was still barely conscious and it didn't occur to him to mistrust her. 'I gotta have that bag. I must. My satchel.'

He got the word out stumblingly. She thought it odd. She'd been on duty when they brought him in and had taken his clothes and locked them up. There hadn't been a satchel.

'My shoulder-bag,' he said again. 'I had it in my shoulder-bag.'

'Not to worry about your shoulder-bag. All your things were taken care of.'

But he was pulling at her hand, surprisingly strong. 'It was in it,' he said. 'I took it with me when I jumped.'

He saw that she was staring but misread her face completely; he thought that she hadn't understood and with the last of his strength said clearly:

'I was personally responsible. The captain for the bomb itself, me for the other thing.'

Bridget started to speak but she saw that his strength was fading. She went for the doctor thoughtfully.

CHAPTER SIX

Martin Dominy went to the hospital again that evening. When he'd called before the place had been a shambles, reporters in the corridors and a harassed American Air Force doctor insisting that his patient was still unconscious. Now Martin hoped for something more positive. He didn't suppose he would have been sent a second time without an introduction, obliged to explain that he wasn't a reporter but had a legitimate but unspecified interest. Russell would have telephoned, smoothing his path. He was experienced at smoothing things.

Martin was shown at once into what seemed to be a doctor's office, but it wasn't a doctor who received him. It was an officer in the United States Air Force. He wore the badges of rank of a full colonel but had Public Relations Officer stamped on him indelibly. 'Please sit down,' he said.

. . . So they'd thought it worth a P.R.O.

The Harvard voice went on politely. 'We've had a message from your chief.' The non-combatant Colonel smiled non-committally. 'Naturally we've heard of him. Will you have a cigar?'

'Too early, thanks.'

'A cigarette?'

The Colonel lit Martin's cigarette. 'If we can help you we'd be pleased to.'

'You'll understand we've a certain interest.'

The Colonel repeated it. 'A certain interest?' His voice was neutral.

'In minimizing embarrassment.'

'There's certainly plenty of it. Plenty of red faces on my side of the table. But the Embassy in London has all that in hand.'

. . . False start. The man was a professional. Martin said smoothly: 'But there's a crew member in this hospital.'

'Whom half the reporters in England have wanted to see. The doctor wouldn't let them.'

'Perhaps that was convenient.'

'I beg your pardon?'

'I meant convenient for both of us.'

'No comment on that from me. Did you expect one?'

'No. But suppose he regains consciousness.'

'May I ask what you'd do yourself?'

'I'd be embarrassed.'

The P.R.O. chuckled. 'Neat. I'd hate to meet you as interrogator if I'd anything to hide. But I'm not going to try to hide things from the Security Executive, especially when you could find them out. In time—that's important. I'm going to give you some news and in twenty-four hours you can do what you like with it. So can the newspapers, who'll also discover it. In the meantime I'm talking to the Security Executive. Secure. Understood?'

'I understand.'

'Then Lieutenant Walter Johnson has recovered consciousness.'

'And talked?' Martin asked.

The Colonel said deliberately: 'He has given his version of the incident.'

'Which I wouldn't dream of asking you.'

It was true. It would have been grossly improper and clumsy as well, premature and maladroit. One should never invite the quite justified No. Martin Dominy pressed his stub out. 'And what will you do when the reporters come back?'

'You tell me. This is England.'

'So it'll also be the English Press.'

The P.R.O. laughed again. 'If you're saying that your newshounds are any slower on a story than our own I wouldn't believe you. But they're sometimes more, well, responsible. The point is to whom. To you—I don't doubt it. A hint from your Colonel Russell and they might very well play along with it, provided, that is, that they all played together. When everybody has a story there isn't a worthwhile story. When it really matters, I mean.'

'You know quite a lot about English newspapers.'

'I worked on one once, the *Gong*. But though they'd play a time-limited ball with *you* they'd raise every sort of newsman's hell if *I* tried to keep Johnson from them. Johnson conscious and talking. The doctors could stall for a day or two, but the longer the stall the more suspicious it would look. The sole survivor held *incommunicado*. That *would* be a story and we couldn't hope to muzzle it.'

'So what will you do?'

'Exactly what you would if the circumstances were reversed.' The Colonel leant forward. 'This is strictly for you alone for twenty-four hours. We're flying Johnson home tonight. For specialized medical treatment in his own country.'

'Very sensible,' Martin Dominy said.

He meant it.

A quarter of an hour later he was telephoning to Charles Russell. Russell said thoughtfully:

'It could mean something or nothing at all.'

'They gave a very good reason for rushing him home.'

'Of course they did. They had to.'

'The man I spoke to was a professional.'

'So you told me—I hadn't forgotten. A professional P.R.O. and not a doctor.' There was a long reflective pause, then Russell said sharply: 'Johnson must have been talking, talking hard.'

'It's a possible explanation.'

'Call it a damned good guess.'

'You'd like me to poke about, sir?'

'Most certainly not. You wouldn't get anywhere, and the last thing we want is to risk the impression that we've been doing some private thinking.' Russell's voice had been emphatic but went suddenly impersonal. 'I think I'll have a chat-up with my useful friend Lord Normer.'

'Lord Normer of Nowhere?'

'Yes. You could call him my blind man's dog, and in matters scientific I'm very blind. Be back at your lodging at ten o'clock precisely. I'll have seen him by then and I'll telephone without fail.'

Russell rang off smoothly, then looked at a jotting he'd made before. There was more to a nuclear bomb than a casing with hell inside it, and one of the aircraft's crew was still alive. Who had now recovered consciousness and they were flying him home for specialized medical treatment. Perfectly credible, adequately explanatory. Up to a point. An admirable, humane motive, but there could also be others. The man would have talked—that was humanly speaking certain. God knew what he'd said but it would certainly have been interesting. And they were sending him back to the States indecently fast.

Charles Russell considered. He had thought when he made his note that it was high time he talked to Lord Normer again; now he was convinced of it and he made an appointment urgently. He walked across the Park to Buckingham Gate.

Lord Normer received him affably. He spent little time in offices, preferring his laboratory or the factories of the company on whose board he so solidly sat. It was an international corporation and it paid him a prince's ransom to keep it straight. He earned it very handsomely, spending development money lavishly but saving more than double on the insidious non-starters which the backroom boys brought up to him. He weighed seventeen stone in his special chair but his little pig's eyes were bright and clear.

'Good evening, Charles.'

'Good evening, Willy.'

'I hope you've not come about bombs again.'

'I'm rather afraid I have.'

'Oh my God.' The enormous jowls sagged in mock dismay. 'I know nothing whatever about the thing.'

'That wasn't my impression before. Last time I asked you how a nuclear bomb was fired. Now I'm asking you who fires it.'

'Charles! You've been reading the paperbacks, going to the cinema . . . ' Lord Normer wasn't pretending now, he was genuinely apprehensive.

'Of course I've done both but you needn't alarm yourself. I don't believe much of what I've read and nothing at all of what I've seen. That's why I've come to you.'

'I see.'

Lord Normer began to explain and Russell listened fascinated. There was nothing secret in this exegesis, only what was deliberately blurred in the interests of public euphoria. Any intelligent non-scientist could have found it out, but it would have taken him more than one question, perhaps a week of false starts and steady inquiry.

. . . So as Russell probably realized the question 'Who fires a bomb?' was in practice the second one. You could put it much more practically by inverting it, asking instead what precautions existed against a bomb being detonated by accident. And that would depend on the political situation at any time. To take an extreme example, remember Cuba. It was a moral certainty that American aircraft had been in the air over Europe and with bombs at the ready—armed. At the other extreme would be a routine training flight, bombs

58

being carried, when they almost certainly wouldn't be fused. The crew might be able to do it if they were told to from the ground, but there'd be a tangle of electronics to unscramble before their cargo came alive. Basically there was a problem here, one for the Russians equally with the Americans. On the one hand they had to reassure us—their allies, the rest of the world for that—that there wouldn't be a holocaust because some aircrew made a bloomer, and on the other they couldn't afford the impression that precautions were so elaborate that an immediate counterstrike would be impeded. Normer didn't credit all the theorizing about a limited response. That was possible if it were an ally which took the first bomb dropped (that damned Frenchman was perfectly right) but drop a bomb on either major Power and it would be scramble all bombers and press everything in sight. Nevertheless there *were* precautions: they were variable but they existed. The mad pilot in a second-feature film was out . . . American pilot decides it's time to smash communism. Steals aircraft and flies to Moscow. Drops a bomb and we're all fried dead . . . No, that was out unless the pilot had accomplices on the ground, and there'd have to be quite a few of them, and skilled. Reassuring? Perhaps. But what you didn't know and would never be told was who held the key to what locks and where, what were his secret instructions and how wide was his discretion both militarily and politically. There was the sleepless night for ordinary men. There'd once been a sort of loaded hint that positively no American bomb could be fired unless the President pressed a button on his White House desk. That was flatly incredible. For certain sorts of rocket perhaps, but for aircraft on forward bases, no. It simply wouldn't make military sense. Lord Normer had sighed enormously. So the original question could now be re-asked. He'd spoken of locks, of a lock on the fusing. The question was who held the key.

Russell digested this deliberately. 'Then every bomb would have some sort of lock?'

'Not would but could.'

'They were sending home a dicy bomb—we agreed on that before. Could it have been the fusing which had gone dicy?'

'I can't say it couldn't.'

'Then let's assume it was that. So a scientist wants to look at it urgently. The fusing's controlled by a lock and the fusing's dicy. Wouldn't your scientist friend want the lock as well?'

'He would, but what the hell?' Lord Normer was irascible. 'What are you getting at? That aircraft broke up and the bomb came down. It didn't explode, so either it wasn't armed or the lock, if there was one, worked.'

'A moment's patience while I blunder on. We're talking on the hypothesis that that aircraft carried both bomb and lock.'

Lord Normer said crustily: '*You* are.'

'Boring you stiff but I'm not yet apologizing. So there was this lock on board and somebody would be responsible for it.'

'Well?'

'One of the crew is still alive.'

'Goddammit Charles, why don't you put your questions to him?'

'I can't.'

'Why not? Has he died?'

'On the contrary, he's at last recovered consciousness, apparently very recently. And they're flying him back to the States tonight.'

'Are they indeed?' Lord Normer said. He was no longer crusty but alert as an overweight sparrow. 'How long had he been unconscious?'

'All the time since the crash.'

'I'm no sort of doctor but it does sound extremely hasty. What's his medical condition?'

'I've no idea and I'm not going to get one. I sent a man to the local hospital but he didn't see a doctor. He was received by a P.R.O. instead.'

'A Public Relations Officer? A professional liar?'

'Willy, you put it crudely. Most respectable profession nowadays. They say so themselves.'

It was Lord Normer's turn to think and he did so quietly. 'It does sound distinctly odd, I'll agree to that. And I'm beginning to catch your train of thought. Oblique as usual and as usual not stupid. You're assuming that there was a lock—pre-set of course, and at the lowest embarrassing if it fell into foreign hands. You could also assume and I'm guessing you have that the survivor was responsible for it. In which case he's either got it still or it fell into the sea with the other wreckage.'

'I'm afraid that's a false antithesis . . . Or it didn't fall into the sea *and* he hasn't got it. Not now. He smashed himself up on landing, remember, and was lucky a poacher found him. In the dark, in a little valley.'

'Charles——'

'Willy, you may relax. I'm not thinking of stealing a friendly Power's box of tricks, but I am assuming this airman had it when he jumped. Now he's come round and he's realized he's without it. So he tells his superior officers——'

'Well again?'

'Who promptly fly him home where they can be certain he doesn't talk publicly.'

'Almost thou persuadest me . . . Then?'

'Then they start a search themselves. Right here.'

'And what's that to you if you don't want their gadget?'

'Think Willy, I beg you—think. I'm decidedly pro-American since I'm alive by their power and favour, but just between the two of us they sometimes rather frighten me. They take risks which we wouldn't—couldn't if you insist on it. Not nowadays. Think of it this way. They've dropped a bomb on our coast and that hasn't made them popular. The fuss is dying down a bit but it wouldn't take much to stir up the dust again. Plenty of people would like to and you know as well as I do just what people.'

Lord Normer said uneasily: 'Your friends might go romping about at night with the Lord knows what apparatus. If anybody saw them——'

'Up goes the balloon again and this time there isn't an answer. No storm to break an aircraft up, no polite regrets for what was obviously an accident. Instead there's secrecy—arbitrary action on somebody else's territory. It'd look highly suspicious too as well as rude. By my personal book I'd do just the same but that's hardly the point if the posse were discovered. Off go our anti-Yanks again and this time they'd have support from quite normal men. There's nothing quite so touchy as a country in a power decline. Worse than an ageing woman.' Lord Normer began to speak but Russell stopped him. 'And there's another aspect which I like even less. Credibility's the word for it. They dropped a single bomb and assured us there was only one, but they drop something else and they don't even tell us. That wouldn't look so hot for the first denial.'

'You think of most things,' Lord Normer said. He didn't sound ironical. 'I accept your apprehensions but I don't accept your facts at all. You haven't really got any.'

'I know. But I've got a *risk*.'

Lord Normer looked at Charles Russell squarely. 'I'm glad I don't have your job,' he said.

It was a comfortable panelled room and the six men round the table were all Americans. It was at least two miles from

Grosvenor Square and apart from the public telephone system there wasn't a connection with the ugliest building in London. Its absence was an essential for the organization which owned the room. It was enormously powerful—some people but not Charles Russell said much too powerful. And it seldom took instructions from United States Ambassadors. It could go higher than that and it mostly did.

Charles Russell had sat in this room himself, on the right of the chairman and not solely as a compliment; he'd sat as a working member of a group of powerful men with common enemies. Today he was absent but his ghost would have been reassured. This was no meeting of wild-and-woollies: these were hard-boiled professionals and like every good professional they thought first of how to cut their risks. The chairman was saying quietly:

'Thank the Lord Johnson remembered it, and for his doctor who told that colonel-man. Who in turn had the sense to ring us promptly. If they'd tried to handle it locally——'

'Or rung the Embassy,' somebody said.

'Men in uniform don't ring Embassies. It's one of the better traditions we've inherited from the British.'

'On whose territory this thing's still lying.'

'And it's certain we've got to recover it. Washington was emphatic.'

'How important do you think it is?'

'Important enough to want it back. They weren't forthcoming on the details but the instruction was unequivocal.' The chairman turned to the man on his left. 'How do you see it?'

'Much as you do, I guess. We could tell Charles Russell and I don't doubt that he'd recover it, but I don't think it would be right to.'

'You mean he might peek?'

'If he said he wouldn't peek I'd accept that blind. But

63

could he give the undertaking? Would it be fair to ask him? And once we'd told him . . . '

'I take the point,' the chairman said, 'so it looks like a job for ourselves alone.' He looked round the table. 'Agreed?' There was a murmur of assent and the chairman nodded. 'Let's get to business then. Each of you has a brief and I propose to run through the contents. First there's a photograph of a small but very delicate apparatus. It may be in a satchel still or it may have fallen out of it. There's a photograph of the satchel too. Next there's an Ordnance Survey Map, one-inch scale. I wish,' he added plaintively, 'we had maps of our own one-half as good. We don't seem to have the trick of it. Johnson came down in a little valley—a combe I think they call it here—and the map reference is marked for you. But I can do better than a map reference. He smashed into a rock, a sort of outcrop, and that's the main feature of the north side of this combe. The sides are otherwise wooded, as you'll see from the last item in your briefs. It's an aerial photograph, and how we got it isn't evidence. Any questions, please?'

'The lootenant had his satchel when he came down?'

'He naturally can't swear to it but he had it when he jumped.'

'It was dark when he landed? A poacher found him unconscious?'

'Yes to both questions.'

'Then it shouldn't be far from the rock which smashed him.'

'That's what we're banking on.' The chairman looked round again. 'Any more questions?'

'This so-delicate apparatus is naturally of metal?'

'Yes. But you're to take the minimum gadgetry because the minimum noise is essential. If you get yourselves seen you've more than half failed, even if you come back with the objective. You can work that one out for yourselves, I guess.'

'I take it we're to go by night?'

'Of course. But I wouldn't count on that too much. This is the English countryside, and you'd be astonished how many people move around in it at night.' For the first time the chairman smiled. 'Poachers, for instance. Greatly to Johnson's benefit but not, I suggest, to yours.'

'How many do we take, please?'

'I think four should do it. At most. Three to search and one as lookout. A single car and hide it well. Take an English one, they're smaller. As few lights as possible but there's a moon after one o'clock.' The chairman stubbed his cigar out. 'And for Chrisake be *quiet*.'

Russell rang Martin Dominy at ten o'clock precisely, unembarrassed by the knowledge that his instructions might sound equivocal. There was a time to brief exactly and there was a time to leave a margin. This was certainly the latter since the margin took most of the page. 'I've been talking to Lord Normer as I said. Who as usual was helpful. But let's take your end first. I suppose you've no further information about that survivor?'

'Only that they're certainly flying him home tonight. The ambulance to the airfield is laid on for eleven-thirty.'

'I didn't suppose they'd lied to you—no motive. But Normer and I thought the haste significant. More accurately, just possibly significant.'

'Of what, sir?'

'I wish I knew that for certain, when I wouldn't be ringing you. But since I am I've got a job for you. You know where that airman smashed himself up?'

'Parke's Combe, they call it. It's a couple of miles from here and difficult to get at.'

'No excessive local curiosity—people going to see the spot? Picnics? All that?'

'There're not a morbid sort of people here and it's too isolated for the trippers.'

'Good. Have you been there yourself?'

'Should I have, sir?'

'No. But could you find it?'

'Certainly.'

'Then do so. By night.'

'And then?'

'You're to keep watch for any visitors. It's also just conceivable that you'll see an object which I can't describe. It would be near the rock which the American smashed himself up on.'

'I'm to bring it to you if I find it?'

'Emphatically not. It's the visitors I'm interested in, not the object I can't describe. The visitors will be searching for the object. I don't know that they're coming but if they do they'll be Americans. I'm interested in whether they come but much more concerned that nobody should see them but yourself. Are you good in the country at night?'

'Not particularly.'

'A pity. Woodcraft is being crafty in woods. But start tonight just the same. Find somewhere close to that rock and hide. Watch and report to me. In no circumstances interfere, and in no circumstances be seen yourself. Is that clear?'

'Perfectly clear, sir.'

Charles Russell put the receiver back. It was very long odds but he was used to accepting them. The Security Executive always covered the really long ones.

CHAPTER SEVEN

Martin Dominy had walked to Parke's Combe at once. His instructions had told him what for the moment was required of him and his training had taught him never to guess at superiors' motives. He had looked at a map and had memorized it carefully. There'd be a moon after one and he'd brought a small torch and compass. He might not be good in the country at night but was confident he could find his way.

Parke's Combe he had heard of but not visited before. It was one of the very few areas still unspoiled, and on a ruthlessly commercialized coast remained a rarity. It could be reached from the shore, but it was a difficult walk over shingle and rocks, even a dangerous walk at certain tides. The beach was a little paradise but few trippers risked it with the paraphernalia of a picnic. Nor was it easily accessible by land. The beach was enclosed by cliffs, broken by the mouth of the combe itself, perhaps eighty yards wide where it met the sea. The combe climbed back from the beach to the land above, its sides becoming shallower as its floor rose steadily, equally steadily narrowing. It emerged in the end into grazing ground, then moor, but the nearest road was at least two miles and there was no track fit for motoring. You walked to Parke's Combe or you didn't go there at all.

Into this still-enchanted combe Lieutenant Walter Johnson had been blown from the open sea, swinging and swaying in the cross-currents from the jagged cliffs, blinded and wholly helpless. He'd missed the cliffs and been sucked up the combe;

67

he'd even missed its wooded sides; but the last of the rocks had caught him, an outcrop staring from the gentler trees. He'd crashed into it and known nothing more.

Martin had come by land, walking by the road from Burke Hoe, then across the moorland. He'd been using his compass often, the torch more sparingly. The moon wasn't up yet but it was brighter than he'd expected, a cool clear night under summer stars. The moor had been rough going, the sour grazing of some hill farm barely more inviting. He hadn't seen a path and there'd been a moment's difficulty finding the head of the combe, but the slope of the ground had funnelled him to it finally. He pushed his way through the bracken and began to descend. It was dark in the thickening trees, a little eerie, but he felt his way down steadily. Soon the trees thinned on either side and he was out on the floor of the combe itself, its wooded sides looming away from him. He couldn't yet see the sea but its smell came sharp.

It took him a minute to find the rock and he used the torch more frequently. It was larger than he'd expected, perhaps thirty feet high, as smooth as glass and naked, quite unprotected by fern or grass, a horrible thing to crash into in helpless flight. He saw that he couldn't climb it but he wouldn't need to try; he'd pull himself up on the scree which surrounded it, then hide in the bushes which crowned the top. It would be an excellent place to hide, a better to spy.

The climb was harder than he'd expected but the bushes ideal as vantage point. The floor of the combe lay spread below and as his night-sight grew sharper so did its outline. When the moon came up he'd be seeing almost perfectly. And hearing as well.

He was hearing already, a little surprised. A townsman, he hadn't expected this. He'd expected a total silence but it was really almost noisy, not a loud noise but continuous, the pervasive tiny stirrings of an English wood at night. He'd settled by now and the night life had accepted him. An owl hooted, another answered; a branch creaked behind him—birds and animals moving, mysterious life. On the floor of the combe there were four of them playing, two parents, he thought, and a pair of cubs. They were grey with white-striped bodies, masks. Badgers. He'd never seen one outside a zoo. He'd passed a hole in the scree as he'd climbed it sweatily. A den, he thought they called it—no, a holt.

He would have liked to smoke but didn't dare. Instead he watched the badgers and waited for the summer moon. He thought. He was waiting for Americans so he thought about America.

He was sound about America since in the Executive one had to be. He was sound and he knew it for his views had been tested carefully. Charles Russell had done it personally and his method had been typical. He'd asked Martin out to dinner and he'd talked to him quite outrageously. Martin had suppressed a smile for a colleague had dropped a hint to him. Russell would keep a score-card and he'd mark it in his own strange way. Agree too obsequiously and you'd lose several marks, but react in shocked astonishment and your engagement with the Executive could end next day. Listen and take it. Pounce on any non sequiturs but don't attack the ethos behind the deliberately provocative words.

They'd been dining in Russell's club over solid claret, and as the level of the bottle dropped Charles Russell's talk grew wilder.

. . . Didn't Martin find it alarming that in a world where peace depended on the balance of terror between two great Powers one of them seemed to be motivated not by the well-tried criteria of power politics but by a personal morality which was nowadays quite out of date? The Little White Church on some smug New England green . . .

Martin had said he took the point but suggested it could be

exaggerated. They might talk like that and some of them did: the late Dulles, for instance—rot him. But when the chips went down they were very tough. Properly tough, reassuringly tough.

. . . But were they? Look at south-east Asia. Did anyone seriously suppose that the Americans couldn't settle it in an hour? Why didn't they then? Why not drop a couple tomorrow and then go home?

There were doubtless sound reasons, domestic reasons. It might be a mistake to suppose that an American President's policy was influenced by anything so ephemeral as a non-existent world opinion.

Another bottle had been opened . . . Damn it, that wasn't good enough. And why not take out China here and now? Why wait till they had the goods and the power to shoot them? China herself couldn't retaliate yet and Russia most probably wouldn't. Publicly she'd scream with rage but secretly she'd be grateful.

Martin had nodded. It was a respectable point in the classic stream of politics and Martin hadn't doubted that a plan to do that existed. Somewhere in the Pentagon and they'd know where to drop to a pin-point. There was only one thing against it and it was historical rather than moral. Preventive wars were seldom successful and never effective for much more than a decade.

. . . Granted with reservations. But the smell of it was frightening still. Americans always insisted that they weren't out to set up the *pax americana*. But they damned well should be.

Agreed. But if they had the power for it they were entitled too to judge the means.

. . . Let's have some brandy.

They'd drunk brandy in the library, Charles Russell talking of other things. He'd been sober as a judge again and he hadn't returned to politics. Martin had guessed his mark at Beta Plus.

He looked down at the floor of the combe again, the badgers were still playing. Suddenly they were not; they'd been there and now they weren't. There was the faintest rustle of movement in the wood on the opposite slope.

Out on the floor of the combe came a single figure. The moon had half-risen, the light was stronger. Martin Dominy stared. He'd been told to expect Americans and for all he knew this was one. But on the whole he didn't think so.

It would have been strange to have sent a woman.

Bridget Deshmukh, born Bridget Macnamee, was brushing her hair in the bedroom of the ugly little semi-detached. There were two beds in it still since she'd nowhere to put the second, and in any case her husband had used the spare room for some time. It was odd, she was thinking—she'd hardly noticed that he had gone. She hadn't expected his death would shatter her but he hadn't left a single trace, not the ghost of a presence and only, with conscious effort, the barest memory. Anthony had evaporated and perhaps that was appropriate. She remembered that Hindus burnt their dead on solemn pyres, the eldest son cracking the skull to release the spirit. Anthony called himself a Christian but he'd been very much a Brahmin still. So had his father. She hadn't refused to have him because he was old and might well be a nuisance, but she simply couldn't face it, not the Brahmin, the race exploiter, not Sir Ganpatrao Deshmukh, K.C.S.I., doubly an exploiter of his own poor kind. This had little to do with her newly-found creed of communism: Sir Ganpatrao flew flatly in the face of every instinct she'd inherited. But poor Sir Ganpatrao, poor Anthony.

Not that either counted against the ineluctable march of history. That was what they called it—she'd looked the word up in the dictionary. She had a peasant's bitter self-respect and she'd never even pretended that she'd been much in love with Anthony. He'd seemed to be contented and for a year or two so was she. She had married him on the rebound. She'd been almost engaged to David Rees or at least she had shortly hoped to be. He was a houseman in the hospital where she'd done her London training and he'd introduced her into the party; he was a Welshman and touchily proud of it, boring her unbearingly with eisteddfods and his grievances —God knew she had her own to bear—and with interminable recitations in an abracadabra he'd called his mother tongue. She'd found out that he'd learnt it privately and to a native speaker of Welsh he was unintelligible. But at least he wasn't English though the manner of her dismissal had been as cruel as any Englishman's. Perhaps, she admitted, crueller. They'd been meeting for several months and she'd had to say no to him. She was a communist now and the bed-thing was unimportant, but an ancestral spark had flared at once, fire and brimstone and her immortal soul. They'd explained that she didn't have one but you could never be perfectly sure.

She'd said no and he had cooled at once, but he needn't have congé-ed her quite so brutally. She'd been walking out of the hospital and so had he. He'd had a girl on his arm and he'd casually introduced her. 'My fiancée . . . '

She'd married Anthony three months later since at least he wasn't English. He wasn't Welsh either and that had helped. All that talk about brother Celts had been tommy rot. Professional Welshmen weren't distinguishable from Englishmen except that they had an accent.

Poor Anthony again. She hadn't been very tactful. Buying that sari and wearing it in the house—that hadn't been considerate. She'd done it as a gesture and she'd hoped he would understand. Naturally he hadn't and the sari had affronted him. He was as Indian as Indian but he wanted to be

English; he wanted to be accepted, God knew why. She hadn't known that when she married him as he hadn't known her private daemon.

Inherited hate—it wasn't pretty. And nor, she knew, was she. She looked in the mirror dispassionately and the Mick-Irish face stared back without self-pity. Her breasts were a size too large. Anthony Deshmukh had deprecated them as un-English but Shripatrao Deshmukh had slyly admired. Her hair was clean but a shocking mess, and a set would cost her money. Not that she couldn't afford it. Anthony had had insurance, much more than she'd suspected: she could live in this house for some years at least and she needn't keep on her nursing unless she wished to. As she did. Two guineas was forty-two shillings though, forty-two bullets for English hearts. Alas that wasn't practical. Not yet. Instead she'd give it to the party.

The party was all she had but it wasn't enough. Not as she stood in it. She didn't suppose she'd marry again, and though she loved nursing she needed more to fill her life. If only they'd take her seriously. All too evidently they did not. She wasn't insensitive, and even if she had been they'd made it clear. She was asked to sell their newspaper, join processions and the protests. They'd take her money but nothing else, they'd implied that she hadn't much else to give. But she'd decided that nor had they. She was shrewd in her fashion and had sensed that they were futile. The local branch was an earnest joke, all the riff-raff of a watering place: a schoolmaster who'd missed promotion, a writer no one had heard of, two painters who couldn't paint. They thought her stupid because uneducated, but secretly she despised them as a pack of dilettanti. Politically they were as effective as the Amateur Dramatic Club.

Bridget brushed her hair relentlessly. So she'd sell the lease and she'd move to London. She knew she'd find work there

73

and she'd join a group which mattered. Activists. People who'd use her and whom perhaps she could use.

But she'd need an introduction if they were going to take her seriously, some proof that she wasn't an Irish clown with a king-size chip which they might sympathize with in public but in private consider un-marxist. She was supposed to hate capitalism, not the English. So she'd need some sort of reference, some key to unlock any worthwhile door.

Bridget had been thinking about Lieutenant Walter Johnson, of what he had said and of what it might mean. She wasn't formally intelligent and she'd been doing her thinking in fits and starts, not trying to force consecutive thought but letting the pieces drop and form a pattern. It was a misty and ragged pattern and an intellectual would have shied from it. But she wasn't an intellectual.

. . . That American had been talking about a satchel he hadn't had. There'd been something inside it and he'd talked about being responsible. He had sounded quite desperate.

. . . So he'd have told his superior officers but hardly that he'd told her too. He'd been barely conscious for a moment and they'd only just pulled him back again. He would scarcely have remembered what he'd said to a nurse half-conscious.

. . . No, but they'd taken her off nursing him. They'd brought in an American nurse, the excuse that she was a specialist. They'd been ponderously tactful but Bridget hadn't liked it.

The kaleidoscope of her thoughts collapsed. She knew nothing of logic and waited for the pattern to reform.

. . . It sounded important, it really did, and whatever it was it was still American. It would certainly be embarrassing if a non-American found it.

The picture was suddenly sharp and clear: 'embarrassing' had focused it. America was the enemy and to embarrass the enemy virtue. If something was lost and Bridget found it

Bridget would move up one and fast. She might even have found the entry into a group which would take her seriously.

She had intended to sleep but dressed again. If she were looking at all she had best look sharp since others could have the same idea. There was nothing secret about where Johnson had come down—all the newspapers had had it. Parke's Combe and she'd been there swimming. Anthony hated the sea and she'd gone alone. There was a rock on the northern side and the American had crashed into it. She put on rubber-soled shoes and began to walk.

From his perch on the rock Martin watched her with respect. He mightn't be good in the country at night but he could recognize the talent. This woman most certainly had it. She made almost no noise, moving with the unmistakable country-woman's walk, not swinging her hips but walking with knee and ankle. She came across the floor of the combe, stopping below the rock.

She began to search, casting like a hound in the open ground, shrugging, then moving to the thicket at the bottom of the rock. This stopped her dead. It was bramble and holly, every sort of English thorn, impenetrable to anything but a gundog. He saw her stand back, apparently considering. The moon had come up full and she raised her face. He caught his breath for it was a face he'd seen. He'd been shown it as a photograph in a file in the Executive.

She seemed to be considering and she seemed to be taking her time . . . No, she was listening. He caught the sound too, the noise of human movement. A man was coming down from the higher ground, a man or men. Martin had heard no car along the road.

Bridget turned on her heel and began to run. She ran heavily but powerfully, well. She was lost in the trees on the other side.

He listened, tensing, wondering if he'd made an equal noise. It sounded like three or four of them though they weren't showing lights or talking. He watched in the cool moonlight as a man emerged at the head of the combe, one man then two more. They stood for a moment silently, accustoming their eyes to the change of light. Then one pointed at the rock and they moved towards it. They moved carefully, fairly quietly, but they weren't in Bridget Deshmukh's class. All three wore brief masks.

They searched the open ground perfunctorily, but Martin could see that the search was formal. At the bottom of the rock they stopped. One pointed at the thicket and for the first time words came up to him.

'Johnson bounced back and they found him in the open. If it's anywhere at all it'll be in there.'

It had been spoken quite softly but in the stillness it carried clearly. It would have carried to the woman too. If she was still in the further trees and Martin could sense her presence there. And Russell had been right again, the accent was American.

One of the men had a pack on his back and began to unship it carefully, another had a plastic pole with what looked like a pad at the bottom. A wire ran from the handle and he connected it to the first man's pack. There was a low-pitched whine which Martin had heard before.

. . . They were going for something metallic with a detector . . .

'Okay. Get moving.'

The second man pushed the detector into the thicket, swinging it from side to side, listening. Nothing. He pulled it out and moved a yard. Nothing but the whine still. He tried again and there was a sudden frenetic clicking. The man said triumphantly: 'Got it.'

'Stand still. Don't move.'

76

It was the third man now and he was putting on gloves. He had wire-cutters too and he snapped them reflectively. He lay down on his face, cutting a painful path through the wicked thorns. They were talking a little louder now but his voice came out muffled.

'We ought to have brought a spaniel.'

'You'll have to do a spaniel's job.'

He emerged at last, feet-first but happy. 'I couldn't find the satchel but I've got what he had inside it.' He had something in his hands, and as he rose they crowded round him. Martin was lying and couldn't see it. Instinctively he inched forward.

With a dreadful deliberation he lost his balance. He knew he was going, he had plenty of time to curse himself, but his weight was now wrong and a fall inevitable. He fought it in silent fury, clawing desperately with his toes. His head and shoulders were too heavy and as he struggled on the smooth rock he slipped again. He'd disturbed a loose stone and it fell with a clatter. The three men looked up.

Martin fell finally, feeling a fool. He'd been taught how to fall and he fell without serious damage, but the thorns had torn him mercilessly. He lay for a moment collecting his wits. He was shaken and cut and he was in the middle of a thorn-thicket. There was an unclimbable rock behind him and on the other side three men in masks. Who'd be curious to say the least.

He'd have to get out quickly or regrettable things might start happening. Such as casually browning the thicket to flush him out. He said stupidly: 'I'm coming.'

He had thought the patch impenetrable but discovered that it wasn't—just. He came out like a snake but he didn't have gloves or wire-cutters. He pulled himself upright finally, an unimpressive figure and humiliatingly aware of it. The three men closed in on him but didn't speak at once. At last one said quietly:

77

'Visitors. We have visitors.' He stared at Martin Dominy. 'And who the hell are you?'

Martin didn't answer him.

'He doesn't look like a poacher.'

'If he is he's a very bad one. All that noise . . . '

The man who'd last spoken was holding something behind his back. The other two moved nearer. One of them flashed a torch.

'His clothes were good. Once.'

'Who are you?' the first man said again. 'How much have you seen and what did it mean to you?'

Martin didn't reply again. He was dazed still and couldn't think of one.

The first man said softly: 'I don't think we dare kill him.'

'No.'

'Whatever he's seen he's seen and we can't undo it. But we can't have him peeking while we deal with the doings.'

'Sure.'

'Okay. Go to work.'

The man on Martin's left moved suddenly and Martin, half dazed still, bought it. He turned sharply towards the left-hand man, his bleeding hands ready.

The man at his back clubbed him cold in the neck.

CHAPTER EIGHT

Charles Russell had been woken at four in the morning by Martin Dominy's telephone call. He hadn't been very angry. For one thing Martin had evidently been more than half concussed still, more loquacious than usual and considerably less lucid, and for another it did a promising young operator no harm to have made a fool of himself. Besides, he had done his job. Putting it at its lowest it must have been humiliating to fall from a hiding place into the arms of the men you were watching, but at least he had watched them and had seen that they'd recovered something. That, to permit a cliché, had been the object of the exercise. Bridget Deshmukh had somehow been present too and that had been unexpected, but it was certainly well to know it since she wouldn't have gone there for nothing.

Russell gave Martin instructions. The Executive's second man was to be told to watch Bridget's movements . . . Which second man? Charles Russell allowed himself a moment of sub-acidity. When Martin had had a restorative sleep he would remember that at an earlier stage of what now seemed to be an ominously expanding incident he, Charles Russell, had sent another man to Burke Hoe on the outside chance that there might be some further danger to Casilda Paine-Pelling. That had been merely insurance, but last night's development suggested rather strongly that it was Bridget, not Casilda, who would now repay attention. Russell hadn't yet withdrawn this second man and Martin would find him in the same small hotel he was using himself. He wouldn't have recognized him as an employee of the Executive since unnecessary acquaintanceship was something it eschewed, but he might have had a drink with him or even a round of golf. He was the bald one, fifty-ish, ostensibly spending the first holiday of his life away from his wife and children. So this man was at once to be glued to Bridget's tail. Martin could now disclose his own position but Battersbee—that was his proper name—was to report to Russell directly. When that had been done Martin himself should go to bed, and if Russell's advice were worth anything he shouldn't, after a rap on the head, eat heavily or drink at all till he had eight hours' sleep behind him.

Charles Russell went back to bed himself. There was nothing more to do for a while and he wasn't a man to pace a room uselessly. This was the end of Act One but it wasn't a one-act play. He wished it were.

He shaved and dressed at his usual time, then walked to the Executive. There was nothing he could do there until Battersbee reported but he'd kept himself sane in a job to destroy nine men in ten by observing a simple but primal rule. It was to keep his private life entirely private. He was accessible at his flat in real emergency but he never took a briefcase home. Now he must consider and he'd do it where he was paid to.

He disposed of the morning's chores and settled to think. A sense of theatre was one thing, something to be grateful for since at least it was a warning, but it helped not at all to foresee developments. And that was his job, his duty if you preferred the larger word . . . A pathetic Indian doctor and an Irish wife obsessed by shadows. The doctor was dead, the wife alive. Russell still couldn't credit that Bridget was a regular agent, but the fact remained that she'd been present at Parke's Combe for some reason he didn't know, and agent or unexplained witness she was still a party member. So unless she was also a perfect fool, always the most dangerous assumption to make about any woman, she'd probably pass on what she'd seen that night. To whom? Russell shrugged. Hardly to her local branch. He could visualize her local branch and his opinion of it was as scathing as Bridget's own. To someone higher up then, very possibly in London where originally they'd hooked her. The branches might be childish but what hovered behind them was quite the reverse. If communism came to Britain, and that wasn't inconceivable, it wouldn't be the branches which stood as heirs to the power and the glory; they would vanish as the Brown Shirts had, as the really hard core took over. A dozen men might perhaps survive but few of these carried cards and no one openly.

Here we go, the old war again. Old and cold too, or at any rate for the moment. There was no sort of guarantee how long.

To whom would Bridget go then? That was Russell's only contact, his only lead. The first man she went to was unlikely to be important, but in the delicate web of conspiracy which miscalled itself a Party every thread was interwoven. She'd slip up to London and somebody would listen to her. The somebody would know somebody else and the somebody else another man. Her story would work upwards and that couldn't be prevented.

And the possibilities of mischief were by Russell's count unlimited. The approach would be simple and the enemy wouldn't muff it . . . Only one bomb had been dropped—*but had it?* In that case wasn't it curious that a party of Americans had been seen at night searching, moreover doing it secretly, which was frighteningly significant. They'd given a formal assurance that they'd only dropped a single bomb, but once before they'd slipped a couple and their first public statements had been, shall we say, misleading. That put it rather generously. So they admit to one in England and a

81

day or two later a posse is searching a wood by night. What should you now believe? What *could* you believe? How safe were these people who hid things from you?'

How safe were you now yourself?

Charles Russell frowned unhappily. It was the seed of suspicion and an expert would sow it shrewdly. Plenty of ordinary people would feel uneasy and not unreasonably. There *could* be a second bomb, there had before, and if a lie had been told it could only have been for a reason. The only reason possible was that this bomb was irrecoverable. So it lay in the Bristol Channel, rotting. Sooner or later there'd be bound to be radiation, or perhaps it wouldn't rot but do something worse. And then? How big was it, what the real danger? Whom could you turn to or even trust when once it was clear that something was being hidden? If these were Anglo-American relations it was high time they were overhauled. It could be puffed up into almost anything if the professionals got behind it.

As Russell was convinced they would. They never threw in their Two-Club hands.

The train of thought was broken by his secretary. She'd been with him for a decade and more and his moods were an open book to her. She saw him, this morning, in rare depression, but it was eleven o'clock and routine was established.

'Shall I bring in the coffee?'

'Yes please, do that.' He had managed a smile but she didn't like the look of it. She brought in the Cona and lit the lamp carefully. He'd pour it when it was ready but she doubted he'd really drink it.

But he drank his black coffee slowly. In putting a tail on Bridget he'd done everything presently possible, but Russell had no illusions. The Party might be impotent but it stood in the shadow of genuine power. He respected power but did not seek it: the little he needed he quietly took. He could be disowned and broken for taking it but he'd known that from the day he joined. They were unlikely to stop his pension and he owned a little money. He wasn't ambitious for honours, he liked his work. Mostly he was a happy man.

He'd have been happier now for some sudden revelation, something better than the knowledge that they'd certainly play their hand out. He could guess to a point but beyond that guessing was futile. It depended who became interested, some earnest rank-and-filer or a man with access to the muscles of power. There was plenty where it was needed and the people trained to use it.

Charles Russell lit his second cigar. Not for the first time he'd have to sit still and wait for it.

It had been a considerable effort for Bridget Deshmukh to screw herself to the point of going to see David Rees again, but it had seemed to her right to do so and a certain moral courage—moral obstinacy if you preferred the term—wasn't something she'd ever lacked. She realized he would have changed since their engagement which hadn't been one, and though she'd made no attempt to keep in touch she'd heard he'd gone up in the medical world. He was in practice now and she knew the address; more important he was the only communist she still knew in London. She caught the early train next morning, pleading urgent private business to her matron.

The practice was in Hampstead, and a woman more worldly would have recognized the ambience at once. Doctor Rees did a little National Health but the bulk of his income was derived from private patients, well-to-do people of advanced progressive views and uneasy in their consciences about the money they'd mostly inherited. It wouldn't offend a man or woman of this world that his doctor was a communist: on the contrary, if he discovered it he would probably rather relish it, privately congratulating himself on his exemplary broadmindedness. Bridget knew nothing of this and, if she had, would have dismissed it as affectation. All she noticed was that the practice seemed both casual and prosperous. She waited modestly in the waiting-room, explaining to the receptionist that she wasn't really a patient but would like to speak to the doctor when his surgery was over. The receptionist had heard this one before, marking a card provisionally: 'Mrs B. Deshmukh. Query: VEN.'

David Rees received her coolly but she could see that she had interested him. She wasn't good with ideas but she was competent with facts and she laid them out with a clarity which a journalist would have approved of. When she'd finished he asked her shortly:

'You're sure you've got this right?'

'Of course I'm sure.'

'Why did you come to me?'

'You introduced me into the Party.'

'But there must be a branch where you live or near it.'

'There is—it's hopeless.'

'I can imagine.' She noticed he'd lost his accent. He considered for some time, at last said guardedly: 'There might be something in this. I can't be sure.'

'That's why I came to you.'

'Have you told anyone else?'

'Not yet.'

'Then don't.' Rees rose abruptly, walking to the door with her. 'I'll keep in touch,' he told her. He saw her out.

He might, she thought calmly, have asked me to tea.

Back in the street she started to walk to the tube station. She'd done as she'd decided to and was going back to Farracombe. She hadn't noticed that she'd been followed. In anything like the country no man could have got near her without her sensing at least his presence but the instinct was inhibited in a town. Battersbee let her get clear, then ran briskly to a call box. He rang the Executive, and since Russell had given instructions was put through to him at once. 'The name,' he said, 'is Doctor David Rees, the address and directory telephone number are . . .'

Russell thanked him and wrote them down. Then he picked up a second telephone and another of the Executive's gears went smoothly into mesh.

David Rees had meshed too, though much less smoothly. He had thought for some time before contacting Kaunas but finally he rang him. He had met Alexander Kaunas through the practice and at first had been simply curious. He seemed to be very well off indeed but to own no profession from which his wealth came. And he wasn't the standard type of the doctor's patients, men and women with gentlemanly but expendable jobs but really living off a patrimony. He had intrigued David Rees who had the curiosity of his blood. Perhaps Kaunas was a criminal, some sort of City con man, maybe even a high-class thief. Rees was a fisherman and had cast his flies with delicacy. Not a bite, not a ripple; not till he'd casually mentioned that his own political sympathies were, well, east of Hampstead. Now he knew all about Kaunas or, disastrously for himself, he thought he did. He rang him up at his country house and Russell listened to him with interest.

' . . . Kaunas?'

'Yes, speaking.'

'Rees here.'

'What can I do for you?'

Rees said intensely: 'Something important's happened.'

'Indeed? With those X-rays?'

Charles Russell nodded briefly but with approval. Kaunas was a professional and professionals were careful with

85

telephones. When some idiot used one carelessly they knew how to handle it.

'X-rays?' Rees was asking. He was obviously puzzled.

'Yes, those plates of my back. The fourth lumbar vertebra, wasn't it?'

'Ah yes, of course.' There'd been three seconds delay and Russell chuckled. It was a mistake to suppose that the Celt thought fast.

'It's important, you say?'

'I think so—very.'

'Then I'll motor straight up and we'll discuss what the X-rays show. I'll be with you in an hour and a half. I take it you'll be in your surgery?'

'I will.'

David Rees had cut off quickly but Kaunas had been slower in hanging up. There was a single word to come still, a muffled aside but clear enough. Kaunas's voice said contemptuously: 'Fool.'

Russell poured himself a mid-morning drink, thinking they'd reached the big league fast. Alexander Kaunas was one of a handful of men on whom the Executive kept standing watch, operators for what in its private jargon it called the Hard Left. Three of them were diplomatists, which by this time didn't scandalize Russell. For by now it was accepted that a man called, for instance, the Commercial Attaché should in fact be a working agent, and the acceptance had compensations for the Executive. Conventions had quietly twined themselves round a system which wasn't conventional: show excess of zeal in your duties of spying and you'd promptly get your knuckles rapped, not necessarily by the Foreign Office which was notoriously *cher collègue* still in the matter of reciprocity, but more likely by your masters who, like all good civil servants, would be horrified by enthusiasm. Charles Russell smiled—the system had advantages for him.

A well-known face might disappear, a reluctant British bumbledom finally obliged to declare it *non grata*, or perhaps recalled by some offended superior; but another would appear quite soon and Russell would know where to find it.

So three of his principal clients were officially diplomatists. Kaunas was not but had a diplomatic background. Russell took from a drawer a brochure covered in boudoir blue— *The London Diplomatic List*. Right at the back with an air of half-apology, half-embarrassment, there was a note which interested him.

List of persons no longer included in the foregoing list but still accepted by Her Majesty's Government as personally enjoying certain diplomatic privileges.

There followed five names, officials of what for a moment had been states but had now been reabsorbed again as Republics in a Union much more powerful. Alex Kaunas's name wasn't on this list since he'd never been more than a trusted clerk. Too trusted by half, Charles Russell thought. He didn't send for the file for he knew the story. When the crash had come the smart Alex had skipped, skipped with three hundred thousand pounds. It hadn't been too difficult with the Legation in total turmoil. The country had changed hands twice, once to the Germans, later and finally back farther east again. Its people had been seafaring, and its shipping associations, family businesses, had used their Legations as other businesses used a bank. There'd been a terrible lot of money and it hadn't been kept tied up too tight. Kaunas was now a very rich man. There'd been law suits but he'd contrived to win.

He was a very rich man but he wasn't happy. The law suits had left an unpleasant smell, and though he'd applied for British citizenship it had somehow always been blocked. In any case the nostalgia of the exile had bitten too deep. He wanted to go home again and he was trying to work his passage. The men who ruled his country now were proud, above all correct: his money wouldn't buy him in but services might and he was rendering valuable services. He pretended to be an exile from a country which had been swallowed: in practice he worked for the swallowers.

And quite without hope that they'd give him what he wanted, which was safe-conduct home to his own grim country and maybe modest employment when he reached it. Kaunas didn't know this but Russell did; he knew because he'd been told so. It was the sort of information which nowadays reached him, part of his highly personal relationship with a senior official sixteen hundred miles to the east. Russell had more than once co-operated in the no-man's-land where their interests weren't actively clashing, and the official, punctilious as were all his race, had punctiliously repaid. Part of that repayment had been blowing Alex Kaunas. He'd never get home, they'd never receive him. Russell could have him and welcome.

So far Russell hadn't since he hadn't had occasion to, but now he considered Kaunas against the background. He despised what was called psychiatry but had a deep respect for other men's minds. He believed he knew his enemies' and he tried to think as they would. With very much larger fish to fry this wasn't the moment to risk an open attack on Anglo-American relations. But open was the important word, because though tactics might change from month to month the basic strategy was immutable. These weren't the men to jeopardize major policy by some ill-considered gamble, but nor were they men to chuck a chance. They'd try to play it both ways, and for that sort of assignment who better than a man you'd already disowned?

Russell finished his drink reflectively. David Rees, he decided, had gone to the worst man possible. He wouldn't

88

know that, but the fact remained. From Russell's point of view the worst of all.

The taxi was driving Rees and Kaunas round the Outer Circle of Regent's Park. The partition between fare and driver was firmly shut and it was an ancient and rather noisy cab. Nevertheless they were talking softly. Kaunas was saying evenly: 'The possibilities for us are enormous. Provided she got it right.'

'I think she did that.'

'I gather you knew her once quite well.'

'Yes, she wanted to marry me.'

It struck Alexander Kaunas, Balt, as quite exceptionally ungallant. He had a low opinion of David Rees and now it fell sharply lower. Nevertheless he could be useful—for the moment he could be useful. Kaunas began to check it off.

'She saw Americans searching, she's sure of that?'

'Quite sure.'

'They found something but she didn't see what?'

'That's so.'

'Then another man falls from a rock and they knock him cold. Did she hear him speak?'

'She heard him speak but not what he said.'

'Accent American?'

'Bridget thought not.'

'Clothes?'

'She wasn't close enough to see.'

'Odd,' Kaunas said, 'it's very odd.' He was compulsively suspicious as good agents were, and this man on the rock was an unexplained loose end. Alex Kaunas was a cautious man, not one to put a foot wrong when a little further questioning was both necessary and possible. He said shortly: 'I'll have to know much more from her.'

89

'She told me she was returning to Farracombe. You could drive there and talk to her.'

'You'll drive there.'

David Rees looked at him, not relishing what he saw. He'd meant to be helpful, to earn praise and perhaps a brief prestige, not to entangle himself in what he now guessed was serious politics. He had a valuable little practice and he didn't wish to risk it. 'I think——' he began uncertainly.

'I do the thinking. You're to go to Farracombe.'

David Rees considered it. After all it would take a day, no more. 'And ask her further questions?' he said. 'What questions?'

'No questions—I'll do the questioning. You're to bring her to my house.'

Rees began to protest at once. 'Impossible, I'm a doctor. Think——'

Kaunas looked at him with a cold snake's eye. 'I think you will do as you're asked,' he said. 'I use the word ask but you'll know the situation.'

David Rees thought it over for he could guess the situation. He'd thought he'd known Kaunas and now it was clear he hadn't. Nothing. He was heartily wishing he'd held his tongue; he said at length:

'But suppose she won't come. She's a very stubborn woman, she really is.'

'You have a point, a valid point.' Kaunas considered in turn. 'Take Mario with you, he's persuasive with women. I'll put him in touch and I'll see that he's properly briefed.'

'Mario Caccia?'

'Yes.'

'I'd rather not.'

Kaunas said icily: 'You'll do as you're told.'

'And what do you mean by properly briefed?'

'Exactly what I said—no more no less. I mean that he'll know what to do if you fail.'

'But I'm a doctor, I tell you. I can't be a party——'

Kaunas stared at him without pity. 'You'll do as you're told,' he said again 'What did they pay you for that princeling's abortion?'

CHAPTER NINE

Alexander Kaunas was one of the very few men on whom the Executive maintained a regular surveillance, but it wasn't a round-the-clock ceaseless shadowing. For one thing there weren't the resources for that and for another the risk would have been disproportionate to any advantage to be gained and therefore, to the Executive, a bad one. But it hadn't been difficult to change gear from a check on movements and contacts to the close watch on his house in Essex which now seemed necessary. There was a shadow on David Rees as well, and though Russell didn't credit that he'd be used for anything active he'd managed to embroil himself and they'd exploit him quite ruthlessly if they saw any profit in doing so. Some chore perhaps, but nothing serious. Bridget was back in Farracombe, where Dominy, for what it was worth, could check on her further movements. But Russell didn't think she'd make any—the main front was now in London. So he had switched Battersbee from Bridget to David Rees. Battersbee was inclined to be self-important but you couldn't doubt his competence. He now had a car and radio and his instructions were to call Russell himself if anything interesting happened.

Who was in his room that evening, wondering how the break would come. Unknowingly he repeated Kaunas's words: the possibilities were enormous but he couldn't even guess at them. He couldn't even eliminate, except for one move which he was certain they wouldn't make. They wouldn't splash it in their newspaper since to do so would be a waste of time. Its circulation was near-invisible and as a newspaper it didn't rank. Its staff was paid the rate for the job but they entered into covenants to pay part of their earnings back again. That meant they had other jobs or private means, and neither was good for a journalist's standing in the cool professional world of working journalists. So splash this story in their newspaper and the others would simply ignore it. It would never get off the ground at all.

That was a single negative, the rest wide open. Russell looked at the clock—it said six twenty-one—and began to lock up methodically. He was brushing his hat when one of two radios on his desk came in. It buzzed for an instant, then the characteristically hollow voice of a short-wave circuit came to him through the static. 'Control? Is that control?'

They were on Send-or-Receive and Russell flicked the switch down. 'Control here—yes.' He let the switch spring up again.

'Jonathan Two calling. I will identify. The word is Mouse.' Russell could recognize Battersbee's voice but played it by the book of words.

'Come in, Mouse.'

'Object of watch left his house at twenty-past five.' The jargon struck Russell as overdone but it wasn't the moment to carp at it. 'I followed him. At five forty-nine he stopped in Portland Place.'

'And then?'

'At five fifty-one another man joined him.'

'Excellent timing, admirable staff work. They spoke?'

'They did.'

'You couldn't hear what was said?'

'No, sir. But the second man was gesticulating. He looked foreign to me.'

'What did he do?'

'He got into the car with the object of watch. They then drove away and I followed again.'

'And lost them?'

'Oh no, sir.' Battersbee sounded offended.

'Then where are you now?'

'In a traffic jam at Shepherd's Bush. I still have the car under observation. Its number is——'

'God damn its number.' Russell was seldom irritable with subordinates but this droning abracadabra had flicked his nerves. 'What's the maximum range of that set of yours?'

'I'm getting somewhere near the limit.' Battersbee added maddeningly: 'The next size up is too big for me.'

'Then if they're headed where I guess they are there's no bonus in your following them. I'll ring another friend of ours. Get off watch and some food.'

'Wilco. And out.'

. . . Wilco, indeed! And out. 'Very good, sir', would have done as well.

Russell picked up the telephone to ring Martin Dominy but after a moment replaced it. It was always a mistake to give instructions too quickly . . . Rees was small beer but there'd been another man with him; he wouldn't be driving west for fun and he wouldn't have reinforcements unless Kaunas had provided them. But reinforcements for what? Hardly for serious action or they wouldn't have let Rees near it, but Rees knew Bridget Deshmukh and Russell could think of reasons why they should want her out of the way for a while. They might perhaps want to question her or they might simply wish to hide her. The former if she was an agent, the latter if she was not. Or maybe a mixture of both. Or keep on assuming that she wasn't an agent. In that case they'd want to be very sure that she didn't repeat her story outside the fold. So . . .

So it was no part of Russell's business to protect one commie from another. Besides, how could he? A twenty-four hour watch on Bridget? That meant eight-hour shifts, two other trained men besides Dominy himself. He couldn't spare them away from London, where the scene had now shifted, through David Rees to a man who mattered. Or send Dominy straight-away to Bridget's home? If she went with Rees voluntarily Martin would look a fool, and if she didn't he'd have to prevent him or look a worse.

Fatal to act at half-cock—fatal and premature. A rather innocent party card-carrier had entangled herself backstage where the real power lay. One could be sorry for her but not take risks. Russell had fiercer game to watch than a woman he felt sorry for.

Casilda Pelling had told Martin that he might call on her again, but he had done so more from duty than from an active desire to see her. She made him more than a little uneasy in a way which he wasn't prepared to define, but she was the widow of a colleague and she was still very low in morale indeed. That was an understatement no doubt, but it was a good deal less alarming than words like revenge or an eye for an eye.

He took her to the fun fair along the coast, hoping that the bustle, the crowd and the happy brashness would cheer her up. As it had for half an hour but scarcely more. Soon she was listless again, too polite to show boredom, but sad and withdrawn as she'd been since Tom's murder. Now she was leaning against the counter of the shooting gallery, watching Martin. He'd just put ten in the black but he wasn't at all proud of it. The two-two had been accurate and at twenty-five feet the range was derisory. The young man running the booth gave him a packet of cheap cigarettes.

'Thank you. I'll have another magazine.'

The young man took the rifle, reaching below the counter.

He came up with a box of rounds but it wasn't the same from which he'd loaded the rifle before. Martin said politely: 'Not those, please.' He knew the form. The rounds would be nicked and if he got five of them on the target he'd be lucky.

The young man said unpleasantly: 'I run this shop.'

'But listen. I'm not interested in cigarettes. I just want to shoot a bit.'

For an instant the young man hesitated, then oafishness won. 'You'll have to take what I give you.'

Martin looked at him indifferently, in no mood for trouble. He hadn't the air of a fairground hand but something of the pedagogue. He was a schoolmaster perhaps, making a little extra in a vacation he couldn't fill. The young man in turn stared at Martin Dominy, not with indifference but with something close to hatred. He could place Martin accurately and in a world he detested . . . Walking stick, neat cap, tweed suit. A country suit! Class uniform, class enemy.

Martin had shrugged and was walking away but Casilda Pelling stopped him. She'd been placing the young man herself, doing a little guessing and as it happened guessing correctly. She pulled at Martin's sleeve as he started to move, her face miserable but determined. Martin Dominy didn't like it; he was English and loathed embarrassments. Casilda said conversationally:

'You don't always work here, do you?'

The boy hesitated again but not for long. He had fashionably progressive views but inescapably was a snob. It wasn't disagreeable to explain that he wasn't a fun fair hack. 'No,' he said almost amiably, 'I'm a schoolmaster. But I'm writing a novel too and I'm working here for material.'

'So you're writing a novel. Let me tell you the plot.' Martin Dominy, slightly sweating now, tried to stop her but unsuccessfully. 'So there's a school of course, and the hero's a young schoolmaster. He has very enlightened politics but the headmaster hasn't. The headmaster is blocking the young chap's promotion. He also has a much younger wife, also of very enlightened views.'

The young man was looking astonished. 'But——'

'As a sort of what-do-you-call-it, sub plot, there's a boy from a broken home. The hero befriends him and there's a hint of you-know-what. All very tolerant, very contemporary. In the end the headmaster dies and the hero gets his wife. But he takes the boy to live with them too.'

The young man had gone red but hadn't commented. Casilda Paine-Pelling did so. 'Muck,' she said simply. 'Tripe.'

Martin Dominy turned to hide a grin. They weren't words he'd heard her use before. The young man was saying uncertainly:

'Are you a publisher?'

'Of course I'm not a publisher, but I read a novel a day to improve my English and most of them are rubbish.' She was meeting the young man's stare, taking in the too-studious glasses, the ragged beard of protest against nothing in particular. 'Certainly I'm not a publisher, but I'll bet you that any publisher could ring up a dozen agents and get a lorryload of that story in half an hour.'

'I hope you're not right. That isn't quite my story but——'

'But it's a very *good* story—turned inside out. Should I tell you what to do with it?'

'Yes, please.' He was puzzled once more but said it.

'So you start with the headmaster.' She'd been cool before but was now ironical. 'He has terribly up-to-date views but his young wife hasn't, and he's holding back the promotion of a very old-fashioned hero. And there's a boy from a broken home still, but he's stupid and impertinent and your hero beats him soundly. The headmaster doesn't approve of that and he tries to break the hero. They quarrel and he pulls a gun——'

97

'A gun, did you say?' It was clearly a very ill-thought-of word.

'A gun. You've got to have some action.'

'You're laughing at me,' the schoolmaster said. He was trying to be dignified and he wasn't very good at it.

'Yes, you could say I am.'

'But I've done you no harm.'

'But you have, you know—indeed you have. You and the damned rest of you.'

Casilda turned suddenly and took Martin's arm. When they were out of earshot he said unhappily:

'That was really a little rough, you know.'

She swung on him in a frigid rage. 'Rough? You call that rough? I'm a widow, aren't I? and you know who killed Tom.'

'But that ass was no communist, just a wet who'll grow up. You seem remarkably good at spotting them but they're not to be taken seriously.' He was trying to be reasonable though privately he was furious with her, but in the event it wasn't necessary. Her rage had gone, she was suddenly spent. 'A communist,' she said, 'or misguided fool.' Her fingers bit unexpectedly into his biceps. 'What's the difference? Tell me that. What's the difference to a woman who's had what I have?'

They walked in silence to his car. He had invited her to supper too, though now he was regretting it, and, knowing that she loved rice, had suggested a Chinese restaurant in Farracombe. But Casilda had firmly declined. Chinese food could be excellent but anglicized Chinese food was flatulent filth and in any case she had rice herself, lean Spanish rice with the kernel not ground out of it. She'd buy a chicken too and they'd eat *paella*. Martin could bring the wine.

He had expected a certain strain after her outburst at the fun fair, but she was Spanish, he was thinking now, the obligations of hospitality inescapable. They'd eaten simply but well, and after supper he sat comfortably, replete and at ease, looking round the living-room. It wasn't what he'd have expected in a broken-down little watering place. There was some furniture native to it, a hideous fretted coffee table topped by a Benares brass tray, but there were also things from her husband's home, fine old mahogany furniture and a Herati rug which Martin could see was a good one. Charles Russell had taught him a little of rugs. He had a bellyfull of *paella* and of a vigorous young Rioja, and the embarrassment at the fun fair had been forgiven if not forgotten. He was in the mood to talk freely, to take anything she threw at him, but he hadn't quite expected what she did. She was brewing coffee on the sideboard, and without turning her head asked suddenly:

'Martin, what's liberalism?' She'd never used his name before.

He said idly, full of good red wine: 'Big L or little one?'

'Is there a difference? I wouldn't know. I once had an English husband but I don't pretend to be English. That's why I asked.'

He considered it as she brought him coffee. From an Englishwoman the question would have been frivolous, or from an intellectual a boring gambit. Casilda was neither but quietly serious. She deserved a serious answer.

'With a big L it's a political party, a handful of men in the House of Commons.'

'The stuffed-handsome one on telly?'

'That's the boy.'

'Who votes for him?'

'Odds and sods on the Celtic fringes, plus a surprising number of others who get annoyed with their own parties but can't quite bring themselves to switch.'

'It doesn't count politically?'

'It doesn't count arithmetically. It can't unless one of the major parties wants its dozen for a majority.'

'Is that how your parliament works?'

'Alas.'

She shrugged, tolerant but not yet interested. 'And with a small l, what's that?'

'That's much more difficult. Call it a frame of mind. There are a couple of clubs in London where you wouldn't get in if they thought you weren't liberal-minded. The food's pretty dreadful at both of them.'

'I asked you a serious question, you know.'

'Yes, I'm afraid you did. You'd need a don to answer it properly, though. At bottom I'd say it was a belief in reason, that the human race is reasonable and that you can improve it through its mind.'

'Fools,' she said savagely. 'Traitors.'

He was less astonished than he might have been since he had an inkling of what Casilda meant. You could come to terms with communism, or if you couldn't then your children would, but you couldn't come to terms with historic fallacy. The humanist error, the great divide. Not the so-called two cultures, the Scientists and the Arts-men, but the liberals and the few realists left. Nevertheless she was certainly over-simplifying. For men of liberal principles just occasionally came to power and in a matter of a month or two *Realpolitik* had captured them, the brute necessity to govern. It always had and it probably always would. Martin said thoughtfully: 'You said traitors.'

'Yes I did.' She shot it at him uncompromisingly.

'But traitors to whom?'

'To all of us. *To me.*'

'I don't think I follow.' He had spoken without considering and at once wished he had. She said with a sort of furious calm:

'They killed my husband.'

He was tempted to let it pass but it wouldn't have been honest. 'It was communists killed your husband.'

'What's the difference?'

He didn't try to answer since he didn't have an easy one. A more devious mind would have put her thought differently, talking about Western civilization, of the common defences now commonly challenged, making a case and quite conceivably a persuasive one. Casilda wasn't devious but that didn't mean she had it wrong. Even if she had, the knowledge wouldn't heal her wound. Her husband had been murdered in the service of the Executive . . . Try to distinguish between the Soft Left and the Hard? A waste of time. Besides, he thought uneasily, he wasn't quite sure he could do so with conviction.

Casilda was mentally sick perhaps, but the damned woman had something. Some sort of horse sense if you looked at it realistically.

CHAPTER TEN

Mario Caccia was a simple Sicilian, except that he wasn't so simple. He was in the Party for what it would give him, which was steady and generous payment for the services he rendered it. They were considerable services for he had considerable skills. Also he was proud of them and Kaunas had offended him. He had a regular means of contact with Alex Kaunas, one proof against tapped telephones and watchers on Kaunas's hideous house, and at a certain hour and a certain place he'd been met by the usual man. He was to pick up a Doctor David Rees and drive with him to a place called Farracombe. From there they were to bring a woman to Kaunas's house. Doctor Rees would arrange the meeting and do such talking as might be necessary, but if talking didn't swing it then Mario was to provide the, well, persuasion. He'd been handed a pistol and a small case of drugs, but when his contact's back was safely turned he threw it contemptuously down a street drain. The pistol he kept since he knew where he could flog it well. In any case he had one, though he didn't intend to carry it today.

He'd been seriously offended since drugs and pistols weren't his tools. Or not on a woman. That wasn't in the canon of a self-respecting southerner. If a woman was unfaithful then of course you took a knife to her, and if she annoyed you by too much chatter then you naturally beat her up. This woman might argue so she stood to take a beating, but Mario mildly hoped she wouldn't. He thought himself good with women and only beat them when he had to. Guns and drugs in a leather case for a job with a woman! All these Nordics were barbarians.

He'd been driven to Farracombe in a total silence. Mario knew with an animal's sense that David Rees was four-letter scared, but it hadn't affected his driving, which was competent and even good. So was the car and David Rees was proud of it. They'd been blocked at Shepherd's Bush at around six-twenty, but the remaining two hundred miles had smoothly vanished in under five hours.

Bridget Deshmukh was thinking of bed when the door bell rang. She opened it in annoyance, hoping it wasn't a man from the local Branch. They had the compulsions of conspiracy and called pointlessly at night. Two men pushed past her silently and one of them was David Rees. The other she didn't know but Rees introduced him. 'This is Mario Caccia, also of the Party.'

Mario took her hand and kissed it, Bridget blushed and took her hand away. She could tell he was a phony and she didn't like the look of him. Rees said pompously: 'We've come about that message you gave.'

For a moment she was exultant—at last they were taking her seriously. But only for a moment. There was something wrong about David Rees and for a moment she couldn't place it, then it came across distinctly, the unmistakable smell of fear. Doctor David Rees was frightened, Doctor David Rees was communicating. Fear. David Rees would be saying one thing but whatever he said he'd be meaning another. She asked neutrally: 'Yes?'

'I've been in touch with a colleague you won't have heard of.' He was as laborious as ever, talking in his new English voice. 'My friend thinks there are considerable possibilities in what you told me, but he isn't clear about all the details. He'd like to ask you some questions at his house.'

'Now?'

'It's important. We can take you.'

She wasn't yet scared but she was humanly annoyed. They might be taking her seriously but they were taking her for granted too. She said firmly: 'No, not now. I'm on duty tomorrow morning and I can't let matron down.' She realized it sounded innocent but it happened to be true. She was a nurse and a conscientious one.

Rees said: 'We've got to take you.' He had blurted it out and she looked at him professionally. She was able to read the signals. David Rees was under pressure and if he broke might do something foolish. For the first time she felt anxiety.

Mario said odiously: 'Come on baby, daddy's waiting.'

He was a horrible little man, she thought, with winkle-picker shoes and absurd *basette*. He was evidently a foreigner and she had her race's massive mistrust of any foreigner. But he wouldn't have come for the ride and he wasn't frightened. It was David who was frightened and . . .

And to confess it so now was she. Playing for time she said again: 'I can't come tonight. Tomorrow——'

'*Subito*.' Mario was grinning at her abominably, his hands in his pockets, smoking a cigarette he hadn't asked her permission to light. He translated, still grinning. 'At once.'

Rees said: 'It's very urgent.' He sounded simultaneously both formal and uncertain. It was a difficult feat but Rees contrived it.

. . . Something's gone wrong, I don't know what. I've done something wrong and they've come to get me.

She was really scared now.

'I'll have to pack a bag.'

'I'll help you,' Mario Caccia said.

'No thanks, I can manage.' She didn't fancy him in her bedroom. 'And I'll have to telephone too.'

The two men exchanged a look.

'To whom?' It was Rees.

'To my matron of course.'

Rees looked again at Caccia and Mario took a reflective drag. He blew the smoke through his nostrils noisily, then spoke unmistakably as the superior. 'Let her telephone to her matron. We don't want her hospital ringing the police when she doesn't show up tomorrow.' He nodded at the telephone. 'But mind, no tricks. And you're not to say where you're going.'

'I don't know that, do I?' She was momentarily calm again for she'd the ghost of a plan to beat them. It probably wasn't the slightest use but it was an outside chance and the only one she could think of. She dialled a number deliberately. It was Casilda Paine-Pelling's.

She knew a little about Casilda because she'd heard it in the local Branch. It had been one of the hopeless painters and he'd had trouble with the Executive, minor trouble as it happened but he'd immoderately resented it. A mild-mannered young man had called on him in London, not threatening him but meticulously polite . . . The painter, who was an official too, had made a contact which he must know was foolish, but unlike many others he could still withdraw from trouble before it hit him really seriously. So the young man's opinion was that he should do so without delay. 'Opinion' put it equivocally but the painter would understand him or if he didn't the civil servant would. He did? That was splendid. Then good day.

The painter had drawn sharply back but he'd been furious and humiliated, and it had been some sort of compensation to wounded pride to pass the story on in his weekend Branch. He'd boasted but he'd protested too. That bloody Executive— it was monstrously getting above itself. The thing had tentacles everywhere, even in Burke Hoe. That widow up on the hill, for instance. What? No, he hadn't got proof, but her name was Paine-Pelling and there'd been that story about her husband some months before. He'd been shot in his bed in Africa and for twenty-four hours the papers had been full of it. Then they'd killed it stone dead and that was odd. That was unlikely to have been because Downing Street had requested it, since the Government wasn't on Old Boy terms with the state where the man was murdered. So if it couldn't have been the official machine it could only have been the other. Why? Because Paine-Pelling had been working for the Security Executive, and the blessings of all good comrades on whoever had knocked him off. His wife? Well . . . But putting two and two together, you know . . .

Bridget Deshmukh had remembered this. She hadn't much considered it but now she must. Put simply they were snatching her and Casilda was her only hope. Bridget didn't dare ring the police since these suddenly sinister comrades might catch a man's voice answering. She was supposed to be ringing her matron. But Casilda must have connections and Casilda was quick on the uptake.

. . . Mother of God, I hope she is.

Bridget finished her dialling and Casilda's voice said: 'Yes?'

'Matron? Sister Deshmukh here.' She'd only just become one.

'Wrong number, I'm afraid. This isn't the hospital.'

Bridget swallowed her heart. Casilda might hang up quickly but it was Bridget's prayer she wouldn't. She was a courteous woman and would wait for a brief apology. Then she'd accept it pleasantly . . .

As Casilda's voice faded Bridget cut in again. 'Matron, I'm so glad I caught you. I can't get in tomorrow, so——'

'Is that Bridget Deshmukh? I thought I recognized the voice. But I'm afraid I'm not the matron, it's Casilda Pelling here.'

'Yes matron, quite. But it's urgent family business and it'll only be for a day or two.'

'But I keep on telling you——'

'I really can't help myself.'

Casilda had been half asleep but there was something about the voice which woke her sharply. She wasn't the matron, three times at that, and Bridget was still ploughing on. She was stupid perhaps but not that sort of stupid. Casilda heard herself say: 'Go on.'

Bridget softly let her breath out: Casilda Paine-Pelling was with her. 'So I'm obliged to leave for a day or two.'

'Obliged?'

'Yes, obliged.'

'Indeed?' A pause. 'Where are you going?'

'I don't know exactly.'

'I see.'

. . . She's got the message, she really has. Not everything, she can't guess that, but she knows that something's wrong here.

Bridget had noticed that the men had begun to fidget and she mustn't push her luck too far. 'I'll ring you again when I can, matron. Good night, and thank you for being so understanding.'

She hung up and turned round. The men were looking relieved but nothing more. She'd got past them, she'd pulled it off. It was up to Casilda Pelling now. 'Now I'll pack,' Bridget said.

'We can give you ten minutes—no more.'

Ten minutes later they were getting into the Bentley. David Rees took the wheel and Bridget sat with Mario in the back. He smelt disgustingly of garlic and the smell had always made her sick. She was feeling sick now but it wasn't the fault of the garlic. For there wasn't a soul in sight as the car moved off. Bridget fought herself stubbornly—it wasn't too late. Absurd to expect a woman to come rushing round at midnight. What could she do if she did? No, Casilda would be telephoning to the important people she knew . . .

Oh God, let her be telephoning.

A wave of garlic engulfed her as Mario burped. She retched but controlled it. Mario looked at her lasciviously, trying to take her hand. The over-bosomed type sent him. She put her hands on her lap and snarled at Mario; she prayed briefly and then was calm. She was going she knew not where and she'd made a mistake. They made you pay for mistakes—she'd heard terrifying stories. Very well then, she'd have to take it since she couldn't do anything else.

Round the world were men with medals which they'd won for a good deal less.

Casilda had been up still but sleepy and grateful for it, thinking of bed. Bridget's telephone call had woken her. She put on a coat and took her bicycle from the shed. She knew the address in Farracombe and it wasn't too far down the coastal road. She made it downhill in nine minutes exactly.

She hadn't stopped to consider but had acted at once. Bridget couldn't speak freely so she must be in trouble. She'd been pretending to ring her matron . . . 'So I'm obliged to leave for a day or two.' 'Obliged' had had an overtone which Casilda hadn't missed, and when she'd asked her where she was going Bridget Deshmukh hadn't known. This wouldn't be some stupid joke—Bridget wasn't the type for them—and Casilda wouldn't sleep tonight with that sort of message to fret her mind. Sleep was hard enough in any case.

She turned into Bridget's cul-de-sac, depressing little semi-detacheds which Casilda instinctively hated. She dismounted at its mouth and hesitated. There was an important-looking car outside the house, and lights in the front bedroom as well as those downstairs. Casilda frowned. Confronted with that important car, the lights and an air of action . . . Walk up to the door and ring the bell? That might be the worst thing possible, even if she could bring herself to do it. If she'd known what she ought to expect she'd go up and ring, but she was a woman, alone, and there was something in the wind which she could smell as Bridget smelt garlic. Like Bridget it made her a little sick. She looked round again uncertainly. The house was twenty yards away and the street lights were on still.

Somewhere a church clock struck twelve. Like a cue in a bedroom farce the lights snapped off.

Casilda began to move again, propping the bicycle against the wall of the nearest garden. She wore the rope-soled shoes of her country and class and she moved up the pavement silently. There was a garage to Bridget's house with a separate gate. She opened it. The garage was in front of her, a clump of privet to the left. She crouched behind it, squatting. Through the ragged untrimmed top she could see the front door.

It opened almost at once and Casilda froze. The hall light was still burning and a thick-set man was the first to come out. He had strong-arm written all over him—the hat, the cocky walk, the sideburns and the flashy clothes. Bridget came next and in the light from the little hall she was white and tense. Casilda began to move for she was Spanish and not a coward.

She froze again as suddenly as a second man followed Bridget. He was as different from the first as a man could be. Casilda could see a worried face as he looked up the short street warily, but it was inconceivable he was a criminal. He hadn't the build, nor the air, nor the dress. He was wearing an old tweed suit, the sort which sat naturally on a man like Martin Dominy. Casilda had thought instinctively of burglars or a stick-up, but if the first man was a hard boy the second most certainly wasn't. He looked remarkably like Martin too, with the same deliberate manner and the air of some quiet profession.

It came to her in a sudden flash: these men were from the Executive. The well-dressed one was the operator and the rough one was his strong-arm. Tom had sometimes gone on jobs like that. Bridget Deshmukh was a communist and they'd come to pull her in. The Executive was the Executive and her husband had worked and died in it. Casilda looked again at the second man. He was carrying Bridget's bag. That settled it beyond shadow of doubt. The Executive was snatching a communist to do God alone knew what to her, but naturally they'd carry a woman's bag. Martin Dominy would have done so and so would Tom. Tom Pelling was dead and Bridget was a communist. It didn't matter what sort of communist. They'd killed her husband.

Casilda watched the car as it drove away, then collected her bicycle, riding home steadily. She'd sleep now, she would indeed . . . A communist and they'd taken her. Casilda believed she knew what that could mean.

Back in her flat she undressed quickly, but there was something she must do before she slept. She started to say her prayers, gabbling them scandalously since she had something important to end with. And you couldn't say that to a man, you really couldn't. But you could to a woman, one who had lost a son.

She began on an Ave and the familiar words came quickly still. Hail Mary, full of Grace . . . She slowed, then said simply: 'And let it be slow and let her suffer. Let her suffer as I have. Please.' She wasn't conscious of any sacrilege, would indeed have been deeply shocked by it. The Queen of Heaven was a woman and a woman would understand her. Perfectly.

She crossed herself decently and got into bed. In two minutes she was fast asleep.

CHAPTER ELEVEN

The radio by his bedside woke Charles Russell with the first of the dawn. It was the men watching Batter's End and a Bentley had gone past the lodge. David Rees had been driving and there'd been a man they hadn't known. There'd also been a woman in the back. Russell thanked them. So that was where they'd taken her. Unfortunate Bridget Deshmukh, misguided Mick: he hoped sincerely they wouldn't harm her. Russell was Anglo-Irish and Bridget's politics were anathema but they happened to have been born under the same incessant rain.

He dismissed her from his mind as he walked to the Executive; he had a more important job to do and he had still to set it up. It was time he had a fruitful chat with his good friend James Scobell.

He made an appointment for after lunch, taking a taxi to Park Crescent, climbing out briskly, paying the driver from the silver he always carried. He was paying a call on the Milton Import and Export Company. They had a fine panelled conference-room where he'd often sat as an honoured guest, but he didn't expect to be conducted to it today. He went up a flight of stairs and pushed a door—the outer office. Russell was conscious that he had crossed the Atlantic. The room was decently warm and a little more, and if anybody drank tea there they had put away the cups. There was an air of brisk prosperity which Russell approved, for this was a front and he happened to know it. But nobody else would. The Milton was a genuine business genuinely paying its way. Russell gave his own name and was taken at once to a smaller room where a man behind a large clear desk had already risen. His hair was black, untouched by grey, though he was almost as old as Russell, and there was a hint of powder round a considerable but well-shaved jowl. He had a fine western whine which it had never occurred to him to mitigate. His vocabulary, yes: on his last trip home they'd laughed at him. But never the whinny. He said in it now: 'Delighted. Please sit down.'

Charles Russell did so. 'It's trouble of course, or I wouldn't be here.'

'Trouble has compensations then.'

'That's really very kind of you.' Russell accepted a splendid cigar. 'I never play poker with people I like. So here it is.'

'I prefer it straight.'

'Very well, you shall have it.' Russell blew a reflective cloud. 'You dropped a bomb on Burke Hoe but in Spain you dropped two of them. Here you've given us formal assurance there was only the one you cleaned up.'

'Don't you believe us?'

'I do. But there are people who'd be delighted if you'd really dropped a second bomb and then denied it. They could use that very dangerously.'

'But they'd need evidence to make it stick. There isn't any evidence because we happen to be telling the truth.' He smiled faintly but finally said it. 'For once and *at* once. We learnt the hard way at Palomares.'

'Then it's a thousand English pities that you've been prowling around at night.'

James Scobell met his stare, the muscular face impassive. 'There are questions I'll have to ask you but one of them I certainly won't. That's "How did you find out?" '

'You were always a good colleague.'

'Thank you, I value that. So that man who fell off the rock was one of yours. And so?'

'As between you and me, so nothing. You've recovered

what you were interested in and I'm not curious for its own sake. I'm here with news and you're not going to like it.'

'Well?'

'My man fell off that rock but saw you.' Charles Russell blew a second cloud for he wasn't without dramatic sense. 'So did somebody else.'

'Oh hell.'

'A woman called Bridget Deshmukh. She's Irish but married an Indian, deceased. She has a certain sort of background but I don't think it's very relevant. What's relevant is that she's a card-carrying party member.'

James Scobell said: 'Christ Almighty.' He'd lived in Europe for many years but communist was still the worst word he knew. 'Why was she there?'

'I don't know that for certain, but she's a nurse in the Farracombe hospital. Where you were keeping Walter Johnson till you wisely decided to move him.'

Scobell took time to think it through. 'It would make life hell for our respective politicians if any of this became public knowledge. We slip a bomb and swear it was a single, but a few days later we're rooting about in an English wood. It wouldn't have been another bomb but there's something called credibility——'

'Exactly the word which had occurred to me myself. But I'm afraid there's more to come.'

'Shoot it while I can take it still.'

'This Bridget is a communist so naturally we've been following up. She took her story up to London to another minor communist. Who then took it to Alex Kaunas. You've heard of Alex Kaunas?'

'I've heard who he works for,' Scobell said grimly.

'He's also been blown. They blew him to me themselves.'

For a moment Scobell brightened. 'Then he's also less dangerous.'

But Russell was shaking his handsome grey head. 'I don't see it like that, I wish I did. Consider the position between us and them, or since I'm not an Englishman let's be practical and say you and them. There's some chance of a sort of *détente* perhaps, and I don't think they want to risk it by doing anything irreversible.' Russell was seldom malicious but for once allowed himself a legitimate dig. 'Nothing like that regrettable aeroplane. But equally they won't miss a chance to foul up our relations, any more than communist shop-stewards pass up a chance to call a strike because the Kremlin's talking to Washington.' Charles Russell shook his head again. 'No, Kaunas is the worst man possible. From our point of view the worst of all.'

'I'm not quite sure I follow that.' James Scobell smiled his pleasant smile. 'You think too fast for a simple man.'

'Rubbish. But I've had more time for thinking and I see it like this. At the level where it matters they won't want to get pushed into attitudes which don't at this moment suit them, but it isn't in their nature to miss a chance as good as this one. Kaunas gives them an option. I repeat the word— option. They'll give him every backing necessary and if he brings it off they'll use it, but if he fails they'll deny involvenent. And it'd be difficult not to accept their word since it was they themselves who blew him.'

'What a bloody awful game this is.' James Scobell thought intently, asking at last: 'You think they'll go for the great big play, for relations between your country and my own?'

'Wouldn't you?'

'I was asking *you*. In all humility. You're a European and I'm not.'

'I think what I told you. They'll play it for both ways.'

James Scobell ground his butt out. 'Do you mind if I pass this to Washington?'

'I wouldn't have told you otherwise.'

'If it doesn't sound an impertinence we'll co-operate in every way.'

'That's what I'd hoped.' Charles Russell rose but Scobell stopped him. 'They'll have to build it up of course—it isn't enough as it stands for permanent damage. You think they will and I'm agreeing with you unhappily. How do you think they'll do it?'

'I wish I knew that, when I wouldn't be here.'

'They've got to start by breaking it. Sometime. Somewhere. If you've any sort of inkling——'

'None.'

Charles Russell found a taxi and drove back to the Executive. He had told James Scobell that he hadn't an inkling but he walked into his room and at once had more. The evening papers were on his desk and his eyesight was still excellent. The headlines stopped him dead in his tracks.

Question Time in the House of Commons was more somnolent than usual. No fireworks were expected today and a regular visitor to the Strangers' Gallery (if an animal so masochistic had existed) would have recognized an air which he'd sensed before, half boredom half resentment, the resentment of an ancient and once potent body now uncomfortably conscious that real power had departed elsewhere. The Chaplain had said prayers in a tiresomely ecclesiastical voice, the Speaker was in the chair, trying to look interested. The Minister of Nuclear Development was up and it wasn't a major Ministry.

She wasn't the House's favourite daughter though she'd once been the glamour girl of the party which she'd then decorated. Now she did not. Ageing Jewesses often achieved an almost unbearable distinction, but the Minister was declining to age. This was a pity. She was showing a little more flesh than a maturer taste would have considered wise in this preposterous

Victorian-gothic palace, and she'd just had her teeth polished. Prominent at any time, this made them look artificial, and to do the Minister justice several of them were not. She was answering Questions about possible nuclear contamination at Burke Hoe. There'd been the customary Whitehall in-fighting as to which Ministry should take them and the Ministry of Nuclear Development had lost. Its Minister was sticking closely to her brief and so far had hit no trouble. Her brief said quite simply that there was no contamination. Civil servants had checked the facts and other civil servants had written the brief. Perfectly predictably it said that radiation was non-existent. Predictably and inevitably.

Whether it was credible would be something for the House.

She was taking a two-part Question now, tackling it smoothly, her confidence growing . . . If the Honourable Member would refer to a previous Answer . . . As for the second part, Her Majesty's Government had received an assurance from the Americans . . .

On the benches behind her Mr Carlyon Canning rose. There was a stir at once for Carlyon Canning wasn't a bore. The House knew all about him, that in most other countries of Europe he'd have sailed openly as a communist, but he wasn't a fellow-travelling nit and he never went off at half-cock. He was in fact good value and by now the House could use some. He stood looking at it tolerantly, superior and aware of it, waiting for the stir to still.

. . . Then was the Right Honourable Lady aware that a matter of days after the formal assurance referred to a party of Americans had been discovered examining the countryside with apparatus? . . .

There was immediate uproar. As a Supplementary Question it was probably out of order, but it could have had the blessings of the Table and still shattered the Minister totally. She stood and gaped. The Opposition was on its feet to the last man there, behind her her own ranks glowered. Some were looking at Canning reproachfully, some sat stolidly and silent. The uproar increased—'Order' and 'Answer'. The Speaker's mouth moved ritually but nobody could hear a word. The senior Minister present had seen something like this before; he knew where to look and did so.

The Press Gallery had emptied like a hen-run with a fox in it and Mr Carlyon Canning, Member for Godshot, was strolling casually out of the chamber.

The editions on Russell's desk had stopped it there but he hadn't any illusions that the later ones would do so. Carlyon Canning would be talking and he'd once been a newspaperman himself; he'd know perfectly what was a story and he'd handle it to perfection . . . No, he couldn't give them names yet, but this was much too serious a matter not to have been checked and double-checked. He'd raised it in the House for just that reason. And yes, his friend from the *Gong* was understanding him correctly. A party of Americans had been seen examining a wood a few miles from where the bomb had dropped. They'd had apparatus and had been using it. Why, in the face of the most solemn of all assurances . . . ?

Charles Russell read on grimly. He knew about Carlyon Canning and he was very much first eleven. So this was the break and they'd take it from here. It wouldn't be difficult, indeed if form was any guide at all it might even be made unnecessarily easy. For somebody in a Press Office would somehow contrive to bungle it, issuing some statement which could be stood on its head by a child of ten. Probability wasn't too strong a word since nobody took service in a Press Office in Whitehall unless they'd first failed rather miserably in the competitive world of journalism. Three depreciated letters after your name instead of money. Russell had seen it too often for optimism. Some office clown would drop a brick, when it wouldn't be just the newspapers but the Press with a capital P. Justifiably it loathed hand-outs and it despised what it called 'tame cats'. It would suddenly be the Fourth Estate, its considerable armament trained squarely on the Government.

And then, when they had them running . . .

Charles Russell sighed.

A coloured telephone rang and he picked it up. Scobell was asking sourly: 'You've seen the evening papers?'

'Yes.'

'And where do we go from here?'

'You tell me that,' Charles Russell said.

Alexander Kaunas had rather more than a suspicion that his telephone was tapped permanently, and since he wasn't without experience he was sure he was now being watched. The knowledge didn't distress him for he could still reach his masters. His contact was officially a Second Secretary, not a senior rank in the orthodox world of diplomacy, but in the world where his real work lay he was something else. Kaunas had been given a rigid schedule of times and wavelengths, and immutable instructions that no conversation was to last more than ninety seconds. He was on the air now, asking a little uneasily:

'What do we do with the woman now that the story's broken?'

'Keep her.'

'A bit of a risk.'

'A bigger to let her go.'

'How so?'

The heavy voice said precisely: 'Think. A man tumbled off that rock, she says, and after interrogation you've believed her. We can guess where he came from but what about herself?'

'She's got a story for that, what she heard in the hospital——'

'Unverifiable. Quite possibly true and quite possibly not.'
'And if it's not?'
'Then she's an agent of the Executive too and what's more you've invited her in. That would have been careless—very.'
'But——'
'Ninety seconds,' the voice said curtly.

It was midnight but Kaunas mixed a drink, then he checked on Bridget Deshmukh before he slept. He hadn't been mal-treating her, simply interrogating her continuously, but he'd kept her door locked at night. Now he turned the key quietly and looked into the room.

It stopped him as a bullet would. Bridget Deshmukh wasn't there.

CHAPTER TWELVE

The papers next morning might just have been worse, but that, Russell thought, was the best you could say of them. No Press Officer had dropped his brick because no Press Officer had dared utter. The only single statement which would bury this story decently would be a firm official denial of what Canning had alleged, but who could now give it or prove the negative if he did? Even that might n >t kill the story dead—not against the background of what was known to have happened before in Spain. Charles Russell frowned unhappily. He wasn't without sympathy for a minister in a corner and he guessed that Canning's Question had been deliberately out of order. So the Minister needn't have answered it, she couldn't have been compelled to. No doubt.

That was totally unimportant now the newspapers were full of it. Eminent political has-beens were writing letters to the editor: this matter needed an answer—now. Leading articles were running it: this matter needed an answer—now. That was in better newspapers, the rest of them were running to form. The *Custodian* thundered pontifically, the *Gong* was angry and xenophobic. Russell managed a smile. It had really been rather clever and he wasn't a man to withhold respect. To break it that way had been a professional's job and so would be the developments. It was those he was concerned with now and he'd called a meeting to discuss them. If himself, James Scobell and Lord Normer of Nowhere could properly be called a meeting. But at least they weren't a committee so maybe they'd get something done. The dog-eared tag was stale but still correct: a camel was a horse for which a committee had done the designing.

They arrived on each other's heels, and Russell put Lord Normer into the largest chair he had. It was still a size too small for him. There was sherry on the round table but also beer. James Scobell took the sherry and Lord Normer a quart of beer. Russell had briefed him already and introductions were unnecessary. Russell tapped on the table quietly. 'Well?'

'I guess we're the cause of this so I'd better start.' James Scobell was piano but not yet defensive. 'D'you think you'll have to ask us the question outright? Confirm or deny we were there at Parke's Combe.'

'We might be forced to. And what would you say?'

James Scobell dropped his eyes. 'They'd ask the Embassy of course, not the Milton Import and Export, and I don't care to answer for embassies.' He drank some sherry thoughtfully. It wasn't his tipple but he could see there was no gin. 'Just between the three of us we haven't been very clever. There was that aeroplane we flatly denied till they kindly produced the pilot, and in the business in Spain we said one thing, then another. I really hate to use the word, but if the politicians and diplomats lie again——'

'You've had it,' Charles Russell said, 'and so have we. Two people saw those men of yours, a man of my own who won't talk unless I say so, but also the Mrs Deshmukh whom I mentioned to you the other day.'

'She's a communist,' James Scobell said sourly.

'Of a sort. But it's a circumstantial story. If Canning presses it as it stands, and that's by no means the only course open to him, then there'd have to be a Commission. The Opposition would hardly stand for less, and you'd be swearing to a lie which is a difficult thing to swear to and make it stick. A mistaken opinion, yes—I grant you that. But a lie . . . ' Russell

121

shrugged. 'I concede the woman's suspect but so, if you make me say it, are some of you. I said some, you'll notice, and meant it. But against the history you've just set out for us——'

'You needn't repeat it.'

'I assure you I wasn't going to. But this I must say for the record between us. If your people were just to deny it, count me out of this completely. There'd be nothing I could do and I wouldn't want to.'

'I'll see that reaches where it matters. Fast.'

'Thank you. So now we can talk. The hypothetical answer would be, "Yes, we were there." If it ever did come to that.' Russell looked at Lord Normer. 'Will it come to the open showdown?'

'I'm not a politician, thank God.'

'That's precisely why I'm asking you.'

Lord Normer considered carefully. 'There's going to be an appalling row, there isn't the slightest chance of avoiding that. But I shouldn't have thought it was beyond the resources of diplomacy to smooth it over.' He destroyed what was left of his quart, turning directly to James Scobell. 'Every trick in the book will be pulled to just that end—to avoid putting your people to the public and final question. Final is of course the working word.'

'And until we reach finality?'

'The appalling row I spoke of.'

Scobell said unhappily: 'But we're ignoring the other side. Finality, you said. Why should they wait for it?'

Charles Russell nodded. 'I'm inclined to agree with Normer that in time the dust might settle. Might. But that isn't at all what our enemies want, so it's certain they'll make the running meanwhile.'

'Then what have we got against us—the order of battle?'

'Canning apart, there's this communist woman Deshmukh

and another party member called David Rees. I know the latter to be small beer and I'm still ready to bet that the woman isn't an agent. But their contact is Alex Kaunas.'

'Bad enough,' Scobell said. 'And behind him?'

'I can't be sure, but there's a Second Secretary at an embassy you'll have heard of. We can't monitor every wavelength round the clock for twenty-four hours, but we've picked up one or two intercepts between Kaunas and this diplomat. If that's what we must call him still.'

'I know who you mean and he's pretty heavy metal.' James Scobell was looking glum.

'The heaviest in this country. He ranks classes ahead of the local Party and would never let them in on anything serious. But he could get top-class non-English backing if he decided he ought to ask for it.'

'To back the option you spoke of, the playing it both ways?'

'I think we'd be wise to assume the worst.'

There was a silence which Normer broke. Charles Russell had briefed him carefully but his profession wasn't security; he said politely enough, but with a hint of his boardroom manner: 'I don't want to interfere in what I don't understand or want to, but it occurs to me that we're missing a point. It all comes back to that bomb, I'm convinced of that.' He looked dispassionately at Scobell again. 'What you did at Parke's Combe or didn't do will be useful to your enemies, but only to the extent that it throws doubt on your earlier statement that you only dropped a single bomb. Whether you're put to the question or not you're going to look impertinent, but we're also agreed that the Parke's Combe affair as such might conceivably die. But if people can be made to think that you really dropped a second bomb, a second which you've abandoned, then all the diplomats in Belgravia will be powerless to stop the rot.' Lord Normer leant forward as far as his bulk and a too small chair allowed him. 'That's what I'd steadily play for if I were this Kaunas or the diplomat-man he works for.'

Scobell didn't answer but Russell did. 'Willy, you put it admirably. And so?'

'You spoke yourself about other courses open to them. So I don't think they've done enough—not yet. They've got to do something more and I think they will.'

'Given this Second Secretary, given the total backing which he could get——'

'I've already taken both of them.'

'Would you care to make a guess then?'

Lord Normer reflected, then answered obliquely. 'Have you thought about radiation?'

'With horror and fear.'

'I meant specifically—a plant. Naturally it would have to be done convincingly. No buying a dead porpoise and touching it up with luminous paint. That's Beta radiation, soft, and any scientist would spot it in ten seconds. But with the resources you're hinting at they could easily do it properly. Ostensibly something from that aircraft which broke up. It gets planted on the shore, apparently washed up there, and is throwing out the hard ones, Gamma . . . So there's something in that channel after all. Contaminated too. The Americans have lied again and we're all at an unknown risk.'

The silence now was for several minutes. Russell refilled the glasses but didn't drink; he said to Scobell at last:

'You think that's on technically? Your own people could do it?'

James Scobell nodded.

'Then it's on for the others. And I don't see how we could stop it if they tackle it from the sea.'

'No. But we might get there first.'

'Collecting whatever they plant on us before some coast-guard or fisherman finds it, before it's taken to a police station or maims it's finder by radiation?' Russell shook his head reluctantly. 'I haven't the men, I haven't the ships——'

Scobell said almost inaudibly: 'I told Washington as you said I could. We might have the ships.'

Lord Normer was suddenly laughing, shaking his seventeen stone in the chair which was too small for him. For a moment it seemed he was going to choke, but he recovered himself and didn't. He said brutally: 'Rule Britannia.'

Batter's End was a hideous house near Colchester. At the turn of the century a retiring Lord Mayor of London had taken the baronetcy which at that time still went with his office and built himself a seat to match. A quarter of what he spent on Batter's End would have bought him any one of a dozen modest manors which lay crumbling round the country-side, unpretentious gentlemen's houses in the fine local beam and plaster. But none of them suited Sir James. He was the head of a family now and the world must know it. Brick and stone were what he wanted, though they weren't the local materials, and brick and stone he could damned well pay for. He built in high Edwardian baroque, a house to raise the hair on sensitive scalps. It wasn't enormous, ten bedrooms perhaps, but every trapping of the pretentious was included with unmatched bad taste—the carriage drive, the gravelled court-yard, the vulgar little clock-tower on the absurdly grandiose stables, the pompous lodge. He built from a full pocket and he built, alas, extremely well. For twenty miles around Batter's End fine houses were falling in sad decay, but this horrible thing would stand for three hundred years and more, an eyesore till somebody pulled it down.

Alex Kaunas had bought it cheap in the early forties, as bricks and mortar undeniably a bargain, and had lived in it ever since. It was a difficult house to run by the sixties, but it had advantages which appealed to him, a certain seclusion and room to keep servants. Alex Kaunas needed servants and they were servants of a special kind.

To this dreadful house Rees and Mario Caccia had conducted Bridget Deshmukh, and now she'd been its prisoner for a day and a night and a day again. Prisoner, she'd decided, was the only word possible. She hadn't been maltreated yet and she'd been given both adequate food and sleep, but she'd been questioned almost continuously for the whole of the thirty-six hours. She'd emerged, if she'd known it, extremely well, since she'd had nothing to hide and no motive to prevaricate, but Kaunas had kept on and on and what had first been her resentment was by now a good deal deeper. Bridget Deshmukh was puzzled but angry too. This was far from what she'd expected, even farther from what she'd hoped for: she'd brought them her story voluntarily but they were treating her like a suspect. She was a simple and honest woman but a proud one and determined. If this was what one found behind the futile local branches . . . This wasn't for her, these *foreigners*. If this was the top she'd dreamt of then she'd be happier at the bottom. Nursing. Nursing on with competence and waiting for The Day. Not the day of Karl Marx, another ambiguous foreigner, but for the day when the English would finally fall, her country at last be one again. To hell with all the rest of it which it now seemed wouldn't serve her cause. To hell with ideas, to hell with the lot of them. They were clever boys, talkers. And how they talked.

And the fact remained they were holding her prisoner. Not cruelly yet and even with a sardonic tact, but she wasn't free to leave at will. They'd made that clear in more ways than one. She was used to regular exercise and had asked to go for a walk. It hadn't been denied her but a man had insisted on coming too, another foreigner apparently who had chattered incessantly about short-wave radio, something she didn't understand or wish to. And they'd been locking her door at night—she'd hated that. She hadn't had a key turned on her since a thoughtless parent had tried it in her childhood. But only once.

And finally there had been that dog. The incident had been too well-timed for accident. Kaunas had received her politely, escorting her to her room. It was comfortable in a plushy way and he'd stood by the window chatting.

'Come and look at the view.'

It had been almost dawn and she'd gone to the window obediently, noticing at once that it wasn't barred. But the drop to the gravelled courtyard was considerable, and as if reading her thoughts a man had appeared from the rhododendrons. He wore the uniform of a chauffeur with black leggings and a leather cap and he was leading an Alsatian on a short steel chain. In the light from the porch lamp he looked up at them and saluted, then walked slowly across the gravel and back into the dark again. The dog didn't look up but padded on.

But now she was ready to go, she'd had enough. Enough of interminable questioning, enough of locked doors and of east Europeans. She knew roughly where she was for she had recognized a village on the journey, a show-place David had taken her to on their engagement which hadn't been one. This house was perhaps five miles from the village and there was a map of the grounds in the downstairs lavatory, the sort of map which hung naturally in a genuine country house with land around but bogus in this villa with its fifteen acres of parkland and dirty grazing. The boundary was marked to the south and she knew where the south lay. The fence ran parallel to a minor road and this road led to her village, which in turn was on a major road where there'd be lorries even at midnight. As for the dog, she wasn't frightened of him at all. She wasn't an Anglo-Saxon and had no feeling that dogs were sacrosanct. There were mounted police who pushed you around and men with dogs to track you down, but she'd seen police horses with broken legs, felled by a bagful of marbles, and police dogs with their guts half out when the broken bottles had done their worst. Poor beasts—she'd been sad. But it was an outrage using beast against man, so if you couldn't take the man you must take the beast.

It was simple: she wasn't English.

There was a writing desk in her bedroom and there'd been a knife for opening letters. It hadn't had any sort of edge and she hadn't tried to give it one, but there'd been pumice-stone in the bathroom and she'd put a respectable point on it. She'd brought nothing of value and didn't bother with her case. All she took was a towel which she tied round her waist.

She let herself down from the window, hanging by her arms. The fall was still formidable and she knew she was taking a risk with it. Twist an ankle and she was done for.

She said a short prayer, let go.

She hadn't been taught to fall as had Martin Dominy; she fell in a heap. For a moment she lay breathless and bruised, then she picked herself up deliberately. She took three steps to the right and three steps to the left . . . Nothing was broken. Good. The porch light was on still and she hugged the wall of the house till she came to its end. Then she slipped across the gravel and the shrubbery swallowed her shadow.

She moved in almost total silence, confidently and at ease. She was in country at night and more than a match for most men . . . Out of the rhododendrons and into an ill-kept wood. Beyond was grazing and the by-road. The clock on the vulgar stables struck the quarter. A quarter past midnight and she'd more than half made it.

Behind her she heard a shout, sensed the glow of the house as its lights came alive. For thirty seconds nothing happened. Then there was a whistle. A dog barked briefly.

Bridget stood still, considering. It was perhaps three-quarters of a mile across the fields to the road, and caught in an open field she'd lose her advantage. She'd have to stand her ground and see it out. It was the dog she must deal with, the man didn't count. She could outrun a puffy chauffeur in leather leggings.

She slipped behind a bush but emerged again thoughtfully. She'd seen something and recognized it, a glint of metal in the starlight which filtered through.

A wave of anger shook her, not her own but all her peoples'. A mantrap, an alien beastliness. The newcoming English who'd raped her land. They'd set mantraps for the poachers and when they'd caught them they'd lashed them raw. A hundred and fifty years ago—what of it? She'd heard stories from her grandfather and he from his father's father. Peasants with starving families, asking no more than the occasional bird or coney, men with legs broken in wicked traps or with faces full of buckshot from the spring-gun they hadn't noticed. Dispossessed men and desperate against landowners who'd owned nothing by blood, colonists, plantation men, the men who set the mantraps. The English. Generations ago? Who cared?

She looked at the trap again. At second glance it was smaller than she'd supposed, not a mantrap at all in the sense of the dreadful things she'd seen in museums, but as a snare for game it was old-fashioned and very powerful. There was a rabbit in it now and she dispatched it mercifully, easing the jaws of the trap but hardly enough to free its leg, feeling with satisfaction that the spring was much too strong to reset by hand. There'd be some sort of key but she didn't have it, so she put one foot on the bottom jaw, the heel of the other foot and all her weight against the second. She did it with care since she didn't want to lame herself. The spring was stiff and potent but the click came at last as the ratchet caught. It would savage a chauffeur's ankle even if wearing leggings. She put the re-set trap ten yards in front of the bush from which she'd noticed it, covering it with leaves, then retreating behind her bush again.

She waited as the man's noise came nearer. The dog was silent but his handler occasionally spoke to him. She had found an L-shaped stick and was holding it in her hand. In the very faint light it could be mistaken for a firearm. The stolen towel she'd unwound from her waist, padding her hand and forearm. The dog would go for the hand as they'd taught him, the right hand which held the pistol. And that would be as she'd planned it.

Bridget Deshmukh was left-handed.

She waited as the man approached, flashing his torch and clumsy. When she had him in line she rose. The dog saw her head and shoulders first, barking once before squatting quietly. The man put his torchbeam on Bridget's face, then bent and unleashed the Alsatian.

'Get her.'

The dog cleared the trap in the first four bounds, the last across the bush and onto Bridget. She'd pushed her hand forward as the curve of the leap turned downwards and the dog took her padded forearm, holding. Her left hand came up with the paper-knife she'd pointed. She knew where the heart was, she knew how to reach it.

The dog released her arm, the dog kicked twice.

. . . Poor beastie, she'd had to do it.

For a moment the man did nothing, then he saw the dog and swore. The accent wasn't English but the idiom emphatically was.

'You bloody bitch. You whore.'

He began to move forward but on the third step stopped dead. He was whimpering softly, shining his torch downwards against his leg. She could see that his leathers had hardly helped: the trap had bitten squarely against the ankle. He dropped the torch and swore again, he pulled with his hands in panic. He could move the jaws an inch as she had herself. It was not enough. As they closed again on the bone he groaned.

Bridget unwound the towel but recovered the knife. She began to run steadily. She ran heavily again, but powerfully, well.

CHAPTER THIRTEEN

The Second Secretary whose grading in his own organization was at least four ranks higher was on the whole well
satisfied. He was one of the quasi-tolerated operators whom
Russell had once reflected on, in theory a diplomatist but in
practice a professional agent, and as a professional he was too
experienced to be complacent. Nevertheless the omens were
good, the tool in his hand exceptionally sharp. The English
weren't the only Europeans sensitive about American power,
more than a little inclined to read its franker manifestations
as blundering affronts to national pride. Which sometimes
they were but by no means invariably. To this admirable
official the distinction was unimportant: Anglo-American
relations would hardly be smoothed by the belief that a
second bomb had been dropped, then indifferently abandoned
after assurances to the contrary, indeed they might barely
ride the storm. His plans followed that premise remorselessly
and he had made them with his usual care.

He would have agreed with Lord Normer that he didn't
have quite enough. Not yet. Carlyon Canning had been clever
—since he wasn't a party member he mostly was—and the
morning papers were reassuring to a man who loved troubled
waters and could fish in them to advantage. What a fuss,
what a meaningless uproar! To a sensitive mind it was genuinely
embarrassing. As if it mattered nowadays what the English
or their Press thought, but reading the English papers you
would think they were still a Power. They weren't of course;
they were dead but they wouldn't lie down. Not that England

was his target since she was barely worth the powder and shot, but her relations with her ally were. Even the greatest Powers weren't quite happy in isolation.

He had made his plan as methodically as a military operation—Phase One, Phase Two, Phase Three. This was Phase One, the shock, the scandal, and thanks to Carlyon Canning it was paying generous dividends. But it was essential to keep the pressure on and that Phase Two would do. Not suspicion or public outrage now, but the hardest sort of evidence that something was very wrong indeed. The diplomats wouldn't smooth off Phase Two—they couldn't. And as for Phase Three . . .

He wouldn't think about Phase Three just yet.

The Second Secretary, since he called himself that in England, nodded. Experience told him that the chances were good, but naturally there were snags and he began to review them. The first was Alex Kaunas himself, for he had a low opinion of Alex Kaunas. The man was a common thief, a renegade too. The Second Secretary knew perfectly well that Kaunas wanted to work his passage, that he wished to return to his native land, hoped to buy himself safe conduct by his services to its masters; he knew also that he never would. This was knowledge and therefore useful, a hold; but he was an old pro himself and preferred to work with others, people on the pay-roll with established ranks and status, not some freelance, however competent.

And just how competent was Kaunas? On his record he was admirable. There'd been that prison job, for example, which he'd handled where a pay-roll man could not. It had been something to snatch a spy from a British prison, spiriting him out of the country before they'd even closed the airports. The Second Secretary smiled contemptuously. In his own country heads would have rolled for that, but here there'd been a shrug and a coat of whitewash. Be that as it may the coup had been a first-class job and Alex Kaunas was entitled to the credit.

What were much less reassuring were his connections with the local Party. The Second Secretary despised it utterly. It wasn't a party in any sense he used the word, but second-class intellectuals, social misfits and parlour pinks, a motley crew of third-rate men with a single thing in common: they'd failed somewhere in the capitalist world before they'd drifted into the Party's net and there wasn't any reason why they should suddenly change to success when in it. He wouldn't trust them with the simplest jobs and had even declined to meet them. When the day came they'd have to be quietly put down but meanwhile they had certain uses. This woman, for instance, wouldn't have told her story if she hadn't been, a member. So you took the smooth with the rough but you watched the rough warily.

It could conceivably be rougher than it appeared. That woman's story was quite extraordinary.

He walked to his stereogram, putting on a record. He had little taste for the composers of his country, preferring the classics, the classical romantics. He put on some Brahms and poured a drink, wallowing sensuously but unashamed. The faintly mongol face relaxed but the trained brain didn't.

. . . An extraordinary story and by its nature unverifiable: she *could* have picked up something in the hospital where she'd been working, she *could* have followed it up for the reason she'd given. Or she could have been cunningly planted to give Charles Russell a needed lead. The Executive were professionals and the Second Secretary another. He respected it accordingly. He would have liked to question Bridget and understood why Kaunas had, but he wasn't entirely happy with Alex Kaunas as an interrogator. He'd never been trained and it was work for the specialist. It wasn't always realized that there were two sides to interrogation: you asked but you also gave. Inevitably. Any question demanded knowledge but it also implied that the questioner had some, and in the hands of the inexperienced it could give away quite a lot. Alex Kaunas knew quite a lot—he'd had to. If Mrs Deshmukh were Russell's agent and he'd been interrogating her unskilfully . . .

They could deal with this woman later but for the moment she didn't matter. He'd told Kaunas to hold her and Kaunas would.

He changed the record reflectively . . . Phase Two was to break in the small hours this morning. Good—the suspense was killing. He couldn't have done what he planned to without reference back to his capital, and they'd been frank with him as they mostly were. Pull off this one and he could name his reward; he could ask for what he wanted and there was something he very much did. He was happy enough in London, there were endless possibilities in a society so clearly decadent, but there was a posting he wanted more, where the real power lay. He could have that for the asking if this broke the way he planned it, but if he didn't bring it off he'd be held to account unmercifully. Fair enough: it was the normal rule.

He allowed himself a second drink, too experienced for optimism but also too experienced not to recognize a powerful hand . . . At round about 0030 and naturally they'd use first-class men. A modest confidence was justified.

Which was in no way shared by Charles Russell and Normer of Nowhere. They were on the defensive and knew it, waiting an attack they could only guess. Russell was saying quietly:

'You still think they'll try to plant something radio-active?'

'Have you a better guess?'

'I haven't.'

'Then suppose they do. What are our chances of getting to it first?'

Russell said uneasily: 'There are a hundred miles of coastline where it could credibly be washed up.'

'And which Scobell's friends have arranged to patrol? It's a pretty tall order.'

'They're pretty tall men.'

'I think you did right,' Lord Normer said. 'To leave it to Scobell, I mean. If you'd had to tell your Minister he'd have had to tell the P.M. in turn. Then the service chiefs and those shellbacks in the Admiralty . . . A flap, a kerfuffle, a G.N.F.U.'

'What's that?'

'When I was a private soldier it stood for grand naval muck-up. Except that we didn't say muck-up.'

'Nor did your officers.'

'Quite. But you think there's a better chance like this? By leaving it to the Americans?'

'We've got to face it, it's still a chance.'

'Care to tell me what they've laid on?'

'I would if I knew but I've been very careful not to. It would have to be done from the sea—we're agreed on that. No more prowling about on the land by either side. And almost certainly at night. I'd imagine that means fast launches and maybe a couple of frigates. Perhaps more but I don't ask.'

'But they'll keep us in touch?'

'They will. I've a competent man in Burke Hoe itself and they'll liaise with him and through him with me. They've made contact with him already, they don't waste time.' Charles Russell smiled dourly. 'We haven't much time to lose, you see. Not if we're guessing right.'

She was flying the burgee of a West Coast yacht club. Her owner wasn't a member but then neither was he British. It wasn't in fact a person at all but the most powerful state which the world had known. A number on her bows had been carefully painted out. She had the lines of an air-sea rescue craft but nothing else in common beyond outrageously powerful engines which would drive her at speeds discreetly unpublicized. Martin Dominy had begged the trip and was talking to her skipper now, a cheerful young man with a Baltimore accent. He wore a fisherman's jersey and shapeless pants, but could have walked about naked and still read *U.S. Navy*.

They were watching the tramp steamer through their night glasses. She was a deplorable object, filthy from stem to stern, flying a notorious flag of convenience. She was also apparently on fire, and under the launch's half-deck the radio operator was receiving her distress signals. He clambered up grinning, a polite Petty Officer but like his skipper not in uniform. The third member of the crew was also looking raffish. They'd been told that they mustn't say sir or salute and so far they'd just remembered. Two stripes was the highest it went tonight. Okay? There'd be an Englishman aboard as well so they weren't to use words which would make him stare. The radio man said with cool contempt:

'She's making a fuss to end the world and on every wavelength there is. She says she's got cotton-seed and it went up unexpectedly.'

Martin Dominy put his glasses down. 'There's certainly a lot of smoke.'

'A lot of lovely black smoke and there's no smoke without fire. Or is there?'

'You don't like the look of her?'

'Not very much.'

'Do you think she'll have seen us?'

The young officer in the jersey pointed briefly at the moon. 'They'd be blind if they hadn't. But they're not trying to signal us. You tell me why not.'

'It's fishy?'

137

'It stinks.' He thought for a moment, then nodded matter-of-factly. 'So we'll cut round behind that headland where there's a beach and a broken-down harbour. They wouldn't try any funny stuff if they saw us lying at anchor there, but it isn't our job to scare them off. So I'm going to slip into a cave I've got marked on the chart. At this tide there seems to be water. Then a camouflage net and Bob's your uncle. They'll think we've gone up the river a bit.' He turned to the coxswain briefly. 'Half ahead.'

They skirted round the headland and in the little bay reversed. The launch slid into the cave stern first. Martin wasn't a seaman but could recognize a professional and this was professional seamanship. They rigged the camouflage net and waited.

'If we climbed along those rocks we could watch the ship.'

'And they might also see us watching them. They'll come, I think—oh yes, they'll come.' The man in the jersey spoke softly again to the radio operator. 'She's still crowding the air?'

'She is. And they've launched the Farracombe lifeboat.'

'Poor bastards, they won't be pleased. It'll be half an hour to get here, though. Enough . . . ' He raised his hand suddenly. 'Listen.'

It was the unmistakable burble of a powerful outboard motor. A boat was coming round the headland and Jersey put his glasses up.

'Pretty smart little craft for a beat-up tramp.'

The coxswain had been watching too as the boat cleared the point in a confident curve. 'Seamen,' he said, 'not Greeks. And two of them.'

'They're towing something,' Martin said.

'Looks like a rubber life-raft.'

'And look at their clothes—protective clothing.'

Jersey said as an order: 'Silence. Freeze.'

138

The outboard came into the bay and approached the beach. Twenty yards from it the helmsman pulled the tiller into his stomach, swinging her into a sharp turn to port, paying out the tow-rope as he did it. The life-raft came round as the turn increased, grounding on the sand at the peak of the parabola. The second man was over the side already, wading quickly ashore and releasing the tow-rope. Jersey whispered behind an oily hand: 'They really think of everything.' The second man boarded the boat again, the first balancing him expertly. He'd taken out the clutch to wait but he hadn't stopped the engine. Now he gunned it decisively. In ninety seconds the outboard had disappeared.

Martin Dominy let his breath out but Jersey was using his own to talk. 'Unship that net. Get the protective clothing out.' The coxswain went astern, returning with four plastic bags. There was clothing inside them and Jersey gave one to Martin. 'Ever worn one of these things before? I'll help you.' He poured Martin into a sort of boiler suit, a hood with a flexible visor, peculiar boots. He changed without help and checked the others, taking the wheel himself.

'Slow ahead.' The engines began to rumble. 'I'll take her as near as I dare, then we'll have to wade. Not to worry.'

'I wasn't worrying.'

'You will.'

There was a Geiger in the cockpit and it began to bleep at eighty yards. 'Mighty strong message,' the coxswain said. He had a boat's lead out and was sounding expertly. 'We can make a bit more.'

'Dead slow.'

The engines' rumble faded. 'Half a fathom. The bottom's rock.'

Jersey cut the engines finally. 'You bring her about while I fetch that thing in.' He turned to Martin Dominy. 'It's your party too—you come with me.'

139

They slipped over the side into three feet of water. The special clothing wasn't watertight but was distressingly heavy to wade in, and by the time they reached the beach Martin Dominy was soaked. He was soaked to the waist in sea water, the rest of him in simple sweat. Jersey shook himself like a dog, then flashed a torch.

'So it *is* a life-raft. One of ours.'

'You're sure?'

The torch shone again briefly but enough for Martin to read it. On the side of the inflated raft were the letters U.S.A.F.

'As you said, they think of everything.'

'More than you know. This is the self-inflating type. It could come down with an aircraft's wreckage and lie on the sea bed for several days. Then a seal on the compressed air could go and she'd pop up like a cork.' Jersey felt in a pocket and produced another Geiger, not the kind with an audible click or bleep; he read the dial frowning. 'I can't take this thing on board—I daren't. We'll have to tow like they did.' He brought a line from another pocket and made it fast to a rubber ring. 'Thorough of them to remove their own. That would have taken a bit of explaining, yes? I mean a piece of best manila on what's supposed to be plain jetsam.'

They ploughed back to the launch, the American paying the line out. The coxswain helped them over the side and the radio operator was grinning again. 'Just fancy,' he said.

'Just fancy what?'

'The fire's under control and they're moving again. All maydays are cancelled and so's the lifeboat.'

'As if we hadn't guessed it.' Jersey turned to Martin Dominy. 'Now we'll tow this thing back to mother.'

'Mother?'

A hand waved at the open sea. 'Mother's out there and waiting, lying low. She's got a cabinful of boffins and they'll want to wash us off. We might even get a drink if we play it cool. Mother's bone dry—she always is—but I'm ready to bet the boffins aren't.' He chuckled. 'One of them's British.'

'I could use a drink.'

'I could use the bottle.'

The coxswain had made the life-raft fast on a line of perhaps a dozen yards. Martin nodded at the trailing craft. 'And that?'

'We've got boffins and a chopper.'

'A helicopter?'

'Right. They'll give it a quick once-over, then they'll let out the air and fly it off. There's plenty of mutual friends will want to see it.'

The Second Secretary was in his office for he hadn't felt like bed before he knew. He'd been promised confirmation by one o'clock and it had come in at 0035. The duty cipher clerk had brought it him and the message said simply, though not in English, 'Done.'

He sighed in satisfaction and rose quietly to go home, but the radio on his desk detained him. The Receive-bulb glowed red and he frowned at it disapprovingly. Only two of his agents could make contact on this most special set and one was out of the country. The other was Kaunas but this wasn't one of his authorized times. The Second Secretary hesitated, but finally decided to answer.

'I am receiving you.'

Kaunas's voice said urgently: 'Something's happened.'

'It should be serious to break standing orders.'

'I'm afraid it is. The woman's gone.'

'I told you to keep her. Explain.'

'She's—she's escaped.'

'When?'

'A few minutes after midnight.'

'Did you try to recover her?'

141

'Yes . . . Yes, of course.'
'Without success?'
'Without success.'
'That is really most regrettable. For you.'
The Second Secretary killed the set.

CHAPTER FOURTEEN

The Second Secretary gave it forty-eight hours, then faced the facts. They were depressing but in his own jargon ineluctable. Phase Two of his carefully scheduled plan had been to land a radio-active life-raft, one with U.S. Air Force markings which could only have been washed ashore from the wreckage of an aircraft, and it could only have been radio-active if there'd been something which had made it so. Another bomb in the sea, a leaker. Palomares all over again but worse. Carlyon Canning wouldn't be needed to publicize that: the British Press would exploit it naturally, the politicians would be up in arms, the curious race known as men of good will, more important by far every sensible man and woman.

And now the Executive had been first to the job and nobbled it. It could only have been the Executive or after forty-eight hours the news would have broken. The Second Secretary sighed. He didn't believe in coincidence, only in rigid reason, and it was easy enough to find one. He'd always been unhappy about Kaunas as an interrogator: he hadn't been trained in what was work for the specialist but in Phase Two he'd been the go-between, a dangerous freelance but regrettably indispensable. So he'd given something away, the fool, and he'd given it to an agent. The latter fact was by now established. The woman's story had always been suspect and now that she'd left (Kaunas's word 'escaped' had been deplorably amateurish) the only deduction possible was that she was an agent of the Executive. A clever one, too. And she'd gone over the wall at midnight, which gave her plenty of time to telephone. Dawn hadn't been till four or five, and there were coastguards to make a search, fast cars and aeroplanes . . .

The Second Secretary smiled grimly. That Executive was very good. It would add to his pleasure to beat it and he still believed he could. Phase Three was still uncompromised since Kaunas hadn't even known of it. Meanwhile there was Kaunas at large himself and Kaunas had dismally failed. Which was sometimes forgiveable, stupidity never.

The Second Secretary sent for Alex Kaunas's file for he intended to open the envelope. It was clipped to the left hand side of the file and was sealed with a seal he respected. The rubric on its face was forbidding but very clear.

To be opened only in circumstances which fall unequivocally within sub-section 117.C.(ii) of the Manual, and then only by one of the officers hereunder named.

The Second Secretary was one of them. He broke the seal.

ALEXANDER KAUNAS. *Reader will already know his background. Stole state funds which, under the shameless English legal system, he has somehow contrived to retain. For several years he has wished to return and has sought to ingratiate himself by acting for us in various ways. His record in these operations has been good to excellent, but Reader will be aware that in no circumstances would he be allowed to return except to prison.*

If this envelope has been correctly opened under the conditions set out on it Reader should now know more.

It has been decided at the highest level that the Security Executive should be informed of Kaunas's connection with us. The reasons for this decision are not here relevant, but Reader must now realize that Kaunas is a blown agent.

144

The Second Secretary whistled softly. He wasn't put out but on the contrary cheered, for he was an official of long experience and could recognize a classic both in music and in his own cold trade. The situation was now a classic one and his use of it should be classical. He began to write it down:

1. *Kaunas is blown and therefore useless in future. Indeed, as things have broken he is a standing liability.*
2. *The woman has already successfully passed on what she discovered from him or guessed at and is therefore for the moment unimportant.*
3. *But Kaunas knows neither of these things.*
4. *Any plan for the future must turn these factors to advantage. I shall accordingly:*
(a) *Instruct Kaunas to eliminate the woman, telling him that this has now been rendered necessary by his own incompetence. He is too experienced to resist serious threats of displeasure, but if he does I may have to make him a specific promise for his safe conduct which I am not in a position to fulfil.*
(b) *That however is irrelevant because I shall simultaneously leak Kaunas's instructions and intention to the Security Executive.*
5. *On that basis the following results will accrue:*
(a) *The Executive may or may not succeed in preventing Kaunas eliminating the woman, but with the previous warning given them they can be relied on to deal with Kaunas himself.*
(b) *Since the woman's cover is work as a nurse at Farracombe she will probably return there. That is an additional advantage. Concentration of the Executive's interest in that area on protecting one of its agents is precisely what we should wish until the whole Plan has fructified.*

The Second Secretary read the last again and smiled. This

was England, the English changeless. There was nothing like a murder to divert their attention from serious crime.

For instance Phase Three of the master plan.

The Second Secretary had been right, though for the wrong reason: Bridget Deshmukh had indeed returned to Farracombe, but for the good and sufficient motive that she had nowhere else to go. On the main road she'd found a lorry and she'd taken a train from London. Perhaps they would try to snatch her again but she had warning now and it wouldn't be quite so easy. She also had a weapon and some knowledge of anatomy. Much courage but no allies at all. She realized this and accepted it. She couldn't go to the police, all her instincts were against the police. Besides, this was Party business and they'd ask her most awkward questions. For all she knew they could jail her and she'd certainly lose her job. She presented herself to her matron, accepting a reprimand which she hadn't earned.

Martin for his part had reported her return, and his instructions had been to watch her: if she left again he was to ring at once. No other instructions had been possible short of second sight by Russell. He knew nothing of a deliberate escape from Batter's End, and hearing that she was back again in Farracombe had taken the simplest hypothesis which covered the facts he'd known, which was that they'd finished with her and let her return. The story she'd brought them had now broken publicly, so why not let her go? Even if she were an agent, and Russell's instinct was still strongly that she wasn't, it was flatly inconceivable that she'd be the calibre to know anything of the life-raft. His men at Batter's End had seen her arrive, but as they hadn't seen her leave she must have been smuggled out in some way unknown. That had been unnecessary, a piece of compulsive secrecy. It was also the sort of thing which Kaunas would do. Russell had shrugged a professional's shrug.

146

In any case Bridget Deshmukh was a minor preoccupation; she was back at her job and Martin Dominy would watch her. Russell had larger worries and the chief of them was the life-raft. He didn't believe that its capture would neatly end it.

This morning Martin was buying blades at the local chemist and the only other customer was Casilda Paine-Pelling.

'Good morning.'

'Hullo, Martin.'

He thought her health had improved sensationally. She was vigorous and alert again, as he'd known her before Tom's murder.

'Come and have a coffee.'

'Love to.'

They went to a cafe, sleazy and depressing but the best Burke Hoe could offer. The coffee was undrinkable and they changed to a pot of tea. Martin said idly, making talk: 'Have you seen Bridget Deshmukh lately?'

'Not in the last few days.' Her manner had changed and Martin couldn't quite place it. She was alert still but suddenly wary; she drank some tea reflectively, then asked outright: 'Why do you ask?'

'I've got a sort of general interest in Bridget Deshmukh. I think you know why.'

'A *general* interest?'

'Nothing beyond that yet. Why do you ask?'

She ignored the question but asked him another. 'Didn't you know she'd left here?'

'As it happens I did.' He was interested now and something more. She was intense again, the gaiety gone.

'Yet you asked me if I'd seen her.'

'Yes, she's come back.'

'She's come back,' Casilda Paine-Pelling said. Her voice had gone suddenly flat and dead. 'You released her and let her come back to Burke Hoe.'

147

'I don't know what you're talking about.' He was out of his depth and resentful that she had put him there. One embarrassment after another . . . He said sharply: 'Come to that, I've a question for *you*. How did you know she'd gone at all?'

'I saw her go,' Casilda said.

'Yet you didn't tell us—you didn't tell me. You knew we had an interest——'

'I thought it was you taking her.'

He considered it carefully, getting nowhere for his pains. He knew she wasn't fooling she didn't fool. 'I think you'd better explain,' he said.

She did so at once without fuss or reluctance. 'Bridget Deshmukh rang me the night she left. She was ringing to me and meaning to, but she was pretending to be talking to her matron, excusing herself for a few days' absence. I guessed she had someone with her, someone who mustn't know she wasn't ringing to the hospital. I guessed she was under—how do you say it?—duress.'

'What did you do?'

'I bicycled to her house to have a look.'

'What happened?'

'There was a big car and two men. One was a very rough type, the other like you. Or Tom. I thought they were the Executive, I thought you were simply taking her.'

'And why should we do that?'

'She's a communist, isn't she?'

He said a little wearily: 'If we snatched every party member we don't agree with we'd need an army. We're not a secret police, you know.'

'Then who were those men?'

'I can tell you that since we know where they took her. They were an ex-boy-friend and a persuader, both from her own organization. The official guess is that they were taking her off to question her. I can't tell you what about just yet. Apparently they've finished and she's returned.'

'Oh God,' she said, 'oh God in heaven.' Her face was a mask of utter grief. The change of mood confounded him but she wasn't fishing for sympathy. She never did. He said quietly:

'I can't leave it like that. I'll have to ask you some questions. I must.'

She nodded but didn't speak; she was pulling herself together.

'You thought something was wrong at Bridget's and you went round to her house to investigate?'

She nodded again.

'Where you saw a large car and two men apparently snatching her. Was there any sort of violence?'

'I saw no violence, I smelt duress.'

'You thought these men were ours and you let her go?'

'I rejoiced,' she said, 'to let her go.'

'But why?'

He wished at once that he hadn't asked it. She picked up her cup with the whole of her hand and instinctively he flinched at it. But she didn't throw the tea at him, drinking it slowly instead. At last she said:

'You're English.'

He was angry now, a natural sympathy eroded. 'I know worse things.'

'Such as savage foreign women who want revenge. Who *need* it.'

She'd never used the word before but now that she had she felt the physical relief of it. He didn't try to answer but took her chair as she rose deliberately. Her face was a ravaged wreck but her eyes were dry. 'Can I take you back to the flat?' he asked.

'I'm not going back to the flat just yet.'

'You don't look very well.'

'I'm not. I'm going back to the chemist since it seems I've another purchase.'

'I could collect it and bring it up.'

'No thanks. I want pills, you know—my sleeping pills.' She looked at him with cold dark eyes, adding with something which might have been stoicism or indifference: 'And for several nights I haven't used them. You see, I haven't needed to.'

He was a man of about forty, carefully dressed in English clothes and employed at an embassy which was neither friendly nor unfriendly. He was by no means the only diplomat in London whose real function bore little relation to his nominal, but this man wasn't just another semi-tolerated agent, another Second Secretary for a Power far less potent. He had built himself a position as the man through whom the leaks came and was accepted and mostly trusted because his leaks were entirely reliable. He wouldn't have lasted a month if he'd been a liar, and he was more than intelligent enough to know it. He enjoyed his position, which was both flattering and profitable, and he was trusted, though with a sane reserve, by such men as Charles Russell and others.

Russell offered him this morning both a chair and his second best sherry. He sipped the sherry appreciatively, hitching his beautiful trousers as he sat down, coming straight to the point since he knew his Russell.

'I've come about Mrs Deshmukh. Naturally you'll have heard of her.'

'Of course.' Russell was promptly interested. His conscience wasn't quite clear about Bridget Deshmukh. His public conscience, yes: it wasn't his business to protect one commie from another, and this he had told himself more than once. And once, he knew, should have been enough. It had not.

Behind his public conscience nagged a private and sensitive instrument. The woman was a fool perhaps, but she had virtues which Russell approved and admired, and she'd tangled herself in business which she was ill-equipped to cope with. He owed her no sort of protection but . . .

'Yes,' he repeated, 'I know Mrs Deshmukh's background.'

'Then you'll know she left Farracombe for a house in Essex.'

Charles Russell nodded.

'May I ask you how you saw that visit? Putting it bluntly, was it voluntary or otherwise?'

'She's a party member,' Charles Russell said.

'And might therefore have gone there voluntarily. Quite. But she didn't, she was forced to.'

'I'd wondered . . . You're sure of that?'

'I've been told to tell you.'

'But she's returned to her hospital—that's already been reported.'

'Yes. She escaped by night. Her hosts pursued her, taking, I may mention, an Alsatian dog to tackle her.'

'With what result?'

'She knifed the dog.'

Russell said to nobody: 'The woman's got guts.'

'She has.'

There was a silence while Russell thought but it was his visitor who broke it. 'I mustn't do your thinking for you but there's an aspect which won't have escaped you. Mrs Deshmukh may be a communist in the sense that she carries a party card, but she was taken to Batter's End against her will and she left it against its owner's. May I ask what you'd deduce from that if you were the owner of Batter's End?'

'That she wasn't a very good communist, no?'

'Nothing more?'

'I'd begin to feel uneasy about her.'

'So have they.'

'Indeed? To what extent?'

'They believe she's your agent.'

Russell's hand went out to the telephone but his visitor's rose and stopped him. 'You do well to act quickly but you should hear the whole story.'

'Shoot.'

'I don't want to sound pompous but I'm obliged to use circumlocutions. So the people on whose behalf I call believe this woman is your agent and that she picked up some information at Batter's End which has been more than normally useful to you. They bear her or you no grudge for that— they're professionals as you are—but they do bear a grudge against the man from whom she acquired it. And that is Alex Kaunas who has apparently let them down.'

'And so?'

'So they've instructed Alex Kaunas to liquidate Bridget Deshmukh. And personally. They insisted on that——'

'But I thought you said . . . '

'——at the same time instructing me that I should tell you of their intentions.'

'Christ,' Russell said, though he didn't swear often. He thought it over quickly though it wasn't very difficult to a man of his experience. 'Thereby writing off Kaunas? Through me?'

'Precisely. Unreliable agents at large are a liability.'

Russell looked at his visitor. There was a question he'd like to ask him but it would be very bad form to do so: he'd lose face and perhaps a relationship which he valued. He said instead: 'A pretty plan.'

'If I may say so without impertinence it might have been born in this room.'

'You flatter us.' Charles Russell was dry. 'And now——'

But the other had risen already. Russell helped him with his overcoat, holding the door politely. He went back to his desk and telephone in three long strides. He was asking for Martin Dominy before his bottom hit the office chair.

CHAPTER FIFTEEN

Kaunas had had a secret and very bad ten minutes with the Second Secretary he answered to. He had hotly protested that he had given nothing away to Bridget, but he'd been faced with a coincidence and been unable to dissolve it. He hadn't been maltreating her but the fact remained that she'd left his house, and a matter of mere hours later Phase Two of the plan had been neatly nobbled. The Second Secretary stuck to the known facts unshakeably. The Executive must have got to the life-raft first and they could have done that only with foreknowledge of its arrival. It followed that they'd had it and it could only have come from Bridget. God knew what else this slyly competent agent had discovered. She'd have to go— the Second Secretary had been adamant. And since the blunder had been Kaunas's he'd be held personally responsible for her elimination. No substitutes, no further risks. He would do it himself or he'd face the consequences.

He'd protested again but not too convincingly since his master had waved carrot before his nose as well as stick across his backside. If he destroyed Bridget Deshmukh quietly he could return to his country at last. He'd known this promise made and broken before, but now there were grounds for a reasonable hope that this time it must be genuine. They could leave him to face the law perhaps, for he'd beaten the English law before and by now had a vast contempt for it; but they could hardly leave him to face the Executive, not after killing one of its people, not when he himself was an experienced and still unblown agent, his knowledge of his masters' plans too great for their peace of mind at night. That was how he reasoned it since he didn't have an inkling that he'd been deliberately blown and was now a cold-blooded sacrifice. But once a killing was even suspected he'd be out in the open finally. Admittedly this was England but the Executive didn't worship at the shrine of the Judges' Rules. They'd break him some way. His masters would have to get him out, for their own sakes, that is, as well as his own. Promises were one thing but mutual interest was another.

He had a vast contempt for the English law but he hadn't yet slipped into dangerously underestimating it. Even in England you couldn't walk up to a woman and shoot her dead: there'd have to be something which could look like an accident. The Executive would suspect of course, but an interest by Charles Russell was his own guarantee that he'd be spirited away before the Executive could break him. Just as he'd done himself with that spy from the English prison, almost certainly by the same tried route. Yes, an accident was the obvious way.

He had gone to Burke Hoe by train with a plan though not a good one, but in the bus from the station a much better had been dropped into his lap. The passengers had been talking about the hospital, and though the accent had been strange to him he'd easily followed the drift. There was a hospital at Farracombe and it wasn't as well endowed as some. So there was a Hospital Day at the Fun Fair down the coast. The proprietors gave a percentage of the takings, and there'd be special stalls selling special rubbish, the Committee and local bigwigs . . .

And the nurses selling flags just like last year.

Alex Kaunas had sighed inaudibly. It would do very well. There were dangerous things at Fun Fairs such as cables whose insulation was a disgrace to the men who maintained them, machinery in deplorable disrepair, shooting galleries . . .

155

Shooting galleries especially. He was competent with firearms.

So was Martin Dominy though he didn't often carry them. This afternoon for once he was, for in any organization less wedded to understatement than the Executive Russell's telephone call would have been called a Red Alert. Bridget Deshmukh was to be protected round the clock and unremittingly. Two other men had left London by car already but until their arrival Martin must cope alone. Her assailant would be Kaunas and he'd be acting on his own; he'd had instructions to destroy her and private motive to do no less. That was enough for the moment—plenty. The inside story, the shadows behind the simple fact, came later. Any questions, really essential ones? No? Then get onto Bridget's tail and fast.

Like Kaunas himself Martin hadn't found it difficult to discover Bridget's movements. A single telephone call to the hospital and he had everything he needed. All the staff less a skeleton would be down at the Fun Fair in uniform . . . All the nurses at the Fun Fair? Yes. It was that sort of Day, it was that sort of do . . . Nurse (you mean Sister) Deshmukh? She wasn't on duty, she'd be there too.

Martin had met Kaunas more than once, but it took him some time to spot him and he didn't begrudge respect when he finally did. The essence of good disguise was a change of stress, not to make yourself conspicuous with dark glasses and phony beards. Kaunas had done this cleverly. Part of his cover was a business which really was one (Martin remembered, allowing a smile, that the Milton Import and Export did the same) and he normally dressed as a businessman in sober suits, a white shirt and expensive shoes. He now wore a panama hat and flannel slacks with a blue reefer jacket a half-size too small for him. The salesman at Hawkes had called it a boating jacket. Wrongly. He'd dyed his black eyebrows grey but that was all. He looked like a prosperous shopkeeper determined to enjoy an afternoon off.

Someone touched Martin's arm and he looked down quickly. Casilda was saying politely: 'Good afternoon.'

He thought she looked terrible, haggard and drawn, but he was more than a little exasperated with Casilda Paine-Pelling. As an intellectual exercise he could just understand what drove her, but a conscious understanding was a mile from a genuine sympathy; he was sorry she was sick still but it was time she made an effort. 'You here?' He spoke in surprise.

'It passes the time.'

His personal instinct was to slip her but he'd been comprehensively trained and he wasn't here personally. Bridget Deshmukh was in danger and Alex Kaunas was here disguised. Casilda couldn't help if it came to any rough stuff but a witness would be valuable if the roughness got really rough. It was an axiom in the Executive that you settled your business privately when it was possible to do so, but when you had to act openly you covered yourself if you clearly could. He said casually: 'Bridget Deshmukh's here.'

'I know—selling flags. I've seen her.' She looked up at him, half indifferent, half curious. 'You're interested in Bridget again?'

'Very interested indeed.'

'You're thinking of pulling her in after all?' There was a hint of contempt he couldn't miss.

'No, someone else is.' His tone matched her own.

'Snatching her?'

'No, killing her.'

She took it so calmly it chilled and repelled him. 'Who's trying to kill her?'

'A communist, a real one.'

'But Bridget's another.'

'Phooey. She's an addlepated Irishwoman whom the Party

157

has attracted. Now she's fallen foul of the ones who matter.'

'And the man who's going to kill her?'

'A hard-core agent.' Martin looked at her, watching closely. 'An enemy. Of mine by trade and of yours by choosing.'

'I'll come with you,' she said at once.

'Very well. Where's Bridget?'

She nodded left. 'Over there with the flags and money box, in uniform.' He didn't spot her at first glance and Casilda pointed impatiently. 'Over there by the shooting place.'

He picked Bridget out from the swirling crowd, perhaps twenty feet from the shooting booth; he picked her out and someone else; he began to run and Casilda ran with him.

'Hurry?'

'Yes, hurry.'

A man in a blue reefer jacket had his arms on the block of the shooting gallery and Martin put himself beside him. He seemed to be shooting quite exceptionally badly. Martin watched him as he fired off nine—two outers, a magpie and six clean misses. Over his shoulder Martin glanced at Bridget Deshmukh. She'd been joined by another nurse and their backs were turned. Kaunas had put the rifle down, staring at the target in apparent disbelief. Martin said softly: 'Don't try it.'

He was sure he could read the game. Here was a man unaccustomed to firearms, certainly not the type to count his shots. There was one in the breech still, the weapon was live, but he'd start handing it to the attendant for a refill. He'd hand it over carelessly, perhaps stumbling as he did so; he'd put out his hand to steady himself, pushing his body round, the weapon too . . .

It was only a .22 but in the head could be fully lethal. Not a shot from the shoulder but at twenty feet at most. A good man might do it more often than not. Martin said again: 'Don't try.'

Kaunas didn't answer and Martin pushed his left hip against him. He carried his gun where his hand fell naturally and he let Kaunas feel it strongly. Kaunas picked up the rifle and fired the last shot, missing. Then he broke the action expertly, handing the rifle to the bearded bespectacled boy who sold the shots.

'I'll take ten more.'

The young man Casilda had unnecessarily mortified reloaded from the proper tray; he gave the weapon back to Kaunas and Kaunas settled his elbows. He fired the ten shots in a single smooth burst.

The black on the target had disappeared as Kaunas put the rifle down. He stepped back and smiled faintly, then turned on his heel. He still hadn't answered Martin.

Martin Dominy turned too, in an immediate dilemma. He couldn't trot behind Kaunas, that was futile and unprofessional, but nor could he stop him somehow trying again. And Russell had been right once more—Kaunas meant serious business. Martin looked towards Bridget Deshmukh. She was chatting with the other nurse and they'd been joined by a man in a bowler hat. He had a ticket on his lapel which said Committee in red letters and he was dressed to go to a race meeting. One of the local bigwigs and showing off. He seemed to be proposing something and the nurses seemed to be doubtful. Martin recognized the manner, the compulsion to be patronizing and the slightly uneasy knowledge that if anything went wrong with you you'd be dependent on these women like any child.

Casilda was at his side still and had turned as he turned himself. She hadn't followed what had been happening and asked quietly: 'What was all that?'

'That was going to be an accident. The man in the blazer was the man after Bridget. There was going to be a shooting accident and there could still be something worse. When a man's really desperate . . .'

159

He didn't approve of Casilda Paine-Pelling but he approved of the way she took it. She didn't waste time on questions but said quickly: 'He's moved over there.' She nodded at a tea stall. 'You could arrest him while he's drinking.'

'Unhappily this is England.'

'Tom always used to say——' she said.

'I can guess what Tom said but we're neither of us policemen.' He was short and a little stuffy, nodding in turn at the nurses and bowler hat. 'Do you know who that man is?'

'I don't but I heard what he said. He's trying to stand them a ride on the Dipper and they're neither of them too keen. I can't say I blame them—Dippers frighten me stiff. I wouldn't ride on one for a thousand pounds.' She interrupted herself uncharacteristically. 'They're moving towards it.'

'Then I'll have to go too.'

'Not me.'

'I wasn't asking you.'

But she was still at his side as they joined the queue. It wasn't a big one, perhaps thirty or forty people, and it would pass through a pay-box into an enclosed wooden corridor. The cars of the Dipper were loaded where it debouched at the other end. Martin said uneasily: 'Once we're in that corridor we shan't be able to see a thing. Our man, I mean—we'll lose him.'

'He isn't ahead in this queue we're in and if he joins it behind we'll see him.' She thought, then added practically: 'He'll have to get on the same car as Bridget if he's thinking of any trouble.' She frowned. 'I suppose they only run one car at a time?'

'I don't know that. I don't think it matters.'

They shuffled past the pay-box and through the corridor. At the end was the loading platform, the rails to the left, a wooden paling to the right. A car was just discharging, the passengers retreating through a separate passage marked Exit. They were laughing or shaken, or shaken and laughing to hide it. Martin said softly: 'The cars hold a dozen. There are eight in front of us including Bridget and her boy friend. Just look behind you casually.'

'No sign of blue blazer.'

'Good.'

He had time for a quick reconaissance and made it. It was the usual Giant Dipper layout. The cars came in almost spent at the wooden platform, where an attendant braked them finally and reloaded. When he took off the brake they slid off again down a gentle slope, making a U-turn to the foot of the hoist. There they hooked in and a cable pulled them up. The rest was gravity, carefully calculated. There was the first and the biggest fall as the car went free, then up again and a swing to the right, then a series of diminishing humps, the track snaking in and out on itself as altitude and speed decreased. Martin decided that the speed would in fact be moderate: it was the curves and the cunning drops which worked the illusion of danger. Those and the minatory notices—*Keep Your Seats, Don't Lean Out, It is Dangerous* . . .

The car before them had loaded and left and Martin recounted the people in front. They were in pairs now, marshalled, a nurse and a stranger at the head of the file, then Bridget and bowler hat, then four more couples. Martin had paid for Casilda but on the platform she'd stood aside. He thought he'd seen her shiver but he couldn't be quite sure. Another woman had taken her place. They began to load.

It happened too fast for deliberate action. A man had come over the paling, dropping heavily but neatly, on his feet. He came straight for Martin Dominy in a quick collected rush. The woman on Martin's right had caught his arm, and in any case he lacked the room for the tricks they'd so painfully taught him. The woman fell to her knees, half pulling him with her, and as he moved down Alex Kaunas kicked up. It was an old-fashioned kick and nothing fancy, but Kaunas had known his target and hadn't missed. Martin collapsed but he put out a foot. Alex Kaunas tripped over it, stumbling forward and clutching the car. The two nurses and bowler hat were already seated. Kaunas hauled himself aboard and struck again. He missed the attendant but he made him step back, releasing the brake as he put up his hands. The car began to move away.

Martin pulled himself upright shakily. The car was slipping round the U-turn and Martin Dominy's legs were water. He tried to rise but fell again. Somebody stepped over him as he came to his knees unsteadily. She began to run down the incline, making ground on the slowly moving car. He saw her face as she boarded it. Casilda Paine-Pelling's face was sick with fear. The car went round the U-turn, gently accelerating, then stopped as another brake checked it at the bottom of the hoist. There was a thump as a rising hook engaged, then the cable began to lift it.

There was a confusion of shouting and swearing and the attendant was doing the swearing. A stranger had taken a swing at him and he was reasonably offended, but he'd been challenged in his position too and was taking it out in bad language. He was waving his arms and protesting loudly, the What-the-hell-do-you-think-you're-doings of the man of some small authority and no capacity to defend it. Martin Dominy paid no attention. He was watching the car as it crawled up the hoist . . . Stop it? The engine was in a shed on the other side. Too far. It wasn't controlled by the man who did the loading and Martin saw no alarm bell. Besides, it might not be wise to try. Kaunas had jumped a queue, used boot and fist, and that would need explanation; but Kaunas was playing for accidents still or he'd simply have pulled his pistol. Martin had felt it hard and cold when he'd been pressing his body against him. So maroon him in a Dipper car and maybe he'd change his mind and fire. You might force him to change his mind and that was rash. On the other hand an accident up there, up there . . .

Martin groaned but not in agony. The pain was still excruciating but his legs were coming back to him. He got himself erect at last, holding the paling helplessly . . . Not on the first rush down, he thought—that wouldn't look wholly credible; but nor would he wait till momentum diminished and the height of the fall with it. The first rush up would be best of all, the highest point on the run but one. The car would still have sway on and the swing to the right was sudden and sharp.

He looked at the car in helpless fury. It was almost up the hoist by now and for a second it teetered, poised. Then the hook disengaged and it started its run. A nurse was in front with an unknown man, then came Bridget and bowler hat, behind them Kaunas. Casilda was in the seat to the rear of Kaunas.

On the platform the fuss was dying down. A lunatic had come climbing in, drunk more than likely or simply one of those queer ones who'd do anything to save a florin. There'd been a sudden affray and a man had been knocked flat, but he was standing by the paling now, very white but it seemed recovering. As for the lunatic they'd deal with him when the car came down. The mood had changed from anger to the easy-going tolerance of an English holiday crowd.

It changed again as suddenly. A woman screamed. The car had come down the first dip fast and was half-way up the slope to the right-hand turn. A man had risen and there were notices warning you not to. He seemed to have lost his nerve, he was shouting and swaying dangerously, and he'd grabbed at the woman in front to keep his balance. Martin Dominy swore impotently. The man was holding Bridget and Martin could guess just how. He had her by the shoulders but high up, at the base of the neck. He'd be feeling for the cavotid . . .

. . . If Bridget gets up she's had it.

163

There was another woman's scream, a frustrated shout. Behind the still standing man the single woman had risen too. She seemed to be trying to pull him down. She was a powerfully built woman and she had him by the elbows, using her weight, leaning back against the upslope. But the man was in a panic now. He had lost his hat and was yelling unintelligibly, but he still had his grip on the nurse in front.

She started to rise unsteadily.

Martin Dominy shut his eyes but forced them open. Casilda had changed her grip on Alex Kaunas. She had an arm across his shoulders now, the first half of a simple stranglehold but apparently laid on innocently. Instinctively he straightened and the car flew into the right-hand turn. Bridget had risen but Kaunas had released her. She fell against bowler hat and he took her weight. Against the turn it was considerable but bowler hat was a solid man. Casilda and Kaunas were upright still and Kaunas had half turned to her. Martin saw her use her shoulder but doubted that anyone else had. It hadn't been obvious, a mere change of balance. She had the ugly heavy shoulders of a woman who had worked with them and centrifugal force was with her. Kaunas staggered and grabbed but Kaunas missed. Casilda swayed too but caught the back of the seat in front of her. Kaunas was clutching at nothing . . .

He disappeared.

There was an instant pandemonium but Martin didn't join in it. Bridget was safe so his business was with Casilda. Some of his strength had returned with the crisis, and as the car slid to rest he took Casilda off it quickly. She was astonishingly cool, the old Casilda. She wasn't visibly smiling but asked him quietly, almost casually:

'I've never been so frightened . . . Is he dead?'

'If he isn't it's a miracle.'

'I've got to be sure, we'll go and look.'

He exploded, and forgiveably. 'Don't be a bloody fool.

There'll be ambulance men and doctors, policemen too. I've got to talk to you first before the police get busy.'

'You needn't worry, I pushed him all right. Did it look convincing, though?'

'Very.'

'Then there's nothing for you to worry about. We'll just go along and make sure he's dead.'

'You're crazy,' he said furiously.

'No, but I was. Not now. I'm as sane as most judges and saner than some.' She looked at him with an innocence more disturbing than any anger. 'I'm well again. I'm clean.'

He stared back at her in silence, his face a mirror to his thoughts. It showed disbelief first, shaded shortly to astonishment, then something not far from plain dislike. He knew that she could read it but she didn't seem to care at all. She went on without changing her look or voice:

'So if you don't want to come with me, all right, I'll go alone.'

But he limped beside her fuming. They had a tarpaulin over Kaunas now and the police were keeping the crowd away. 'They'll want a statement from you later,' he told her grimly.

'You assured me it looked convincing so I'll give them a beautiful statement.' She looked at the tarpaulin, dropped her voice a half-tone lower. 'Was he really a communist agent? I mean a really important one?'

'One of the very top men.'

'A killer?'

'Yes.'

'That's much more satisfactory than a stooge like Bridget Deshmukh.'

'You really mean satisfactory?'

'No, I think I meant satisfying . . . Do you read the Old Testament?'

'Not very often.'

'You should, you know—it was often right.' She took his arm gaily. 'Now I'll buy you a drink before the police start in on both of us.'

CHAPTER SIXTEEN

The clans had gathered discreetly in the fine panelled room which the Milton Import and Export company ironically called its boardroom, the instinct of each man present that whichever way it now happened to break this was the final showdown. The chairman was American, and in Russell's opinion naturally, since nobody round the table believed that the end of the road had been reached with the death of Kaunas, and the resources to block any further move must inevitably be American. This powerful but retiring man had flown in that morning from Washington. There were people who disapproved of him but Russell didn't share their view. When exposed to brute *Realpolitik* he was happy enough to do business with an unquestioned real politician.

He was happy for other reasons too, for he'd been to see his Minister. His Minister had joined his party in the flush of a youthful idealism and after forty years' solid service thought its principles idiotic. It was an opinion he never publicly aired since it would promptly have lost him his Cabinet job. Whereupon some young enthusiast would step into his shoes, whereupon there'd be many changes of the sort which all practical men deplored. He was an excellent working Minister and got on easily with Russell. More important he had won his trust. He had listened attentively, then smoked most of a cigarette with a mug of quite lethal tea . . . Was Russell insisting that his report should go on paper? The American involvement in particular? No? Then the Minister had forgotten it unless and until it should be necessary to remember.

And the best of British luck to them all. They were probably going to need it.

So Russell was sitting in the Milton Import and Export's boardroom, happily taking instructions from an American he admired. Not that this American was the type to bark his orders. He was in fact doing the opposite, trying to draw Charles Russell out; he was asking him with grave courtesy:

'Then how do you now see it?'

'Since you ask me I think we can eliminate one guess. Our enemies must know by now that we got to that life-raft first. So if we weren't on notice previously we're certainly on notice now.'

'Quite so. But on notice of what?'

'I see it first not as what but whether. Will they in fact go further?' Russell looked round the table. 'Anyone care to help me out?'

'I'd like to ask you a question, please.' It was James Scobell and Russell nodded. 'You told me before that you'd been picking up intercepts, chats between Kaunas and a certain Second Secretary.'

'Unhappily nothing which bears on this.'

'But you're certain they've been in touch?'

'Quite sure.'

'That man has the power to try again and I think he's the kind to do so.'

'I think so too.'

The chairman came in again. 'And there's evidence, though negative, that he intends to do just that.' He looked again at Russell. 'That double cross on Kaunas which ended in, er, an accident. Anything strike you about it—anything odd?'

'It struck me as misplaced. Even for a man who's allegedly a diplomatist.'

The chairman nodded approvingly. He'd had a tiring flight from Washington but his manners were unimpaired. 'I see that we're thinking alike. It's a classic ploy to send a blown agent on a murder, then warn your opposition of exactly what he intends, but if I'd been this Second Secretary I doubt if I'd have employed it in this particular case. Why should I? Wouldn't it have been simpler to let Kaunas return to his country? After all, that was what he wanted, and once there he could have disappeared without a soul in the land the wiser.'

'From which you deduce?'

'Deduction's too strong but there's a guess which fits the facts. The intention was to distract us, I think—to give us the impression that the life-raft plant was final. Since an agent had let him down in that our so-amiable Second Secretary was mopping up an un-success.' The chairman held a hand up. 'Finish—the classic end.' He dropped the hand. 'I mean that he hoped we'd think like that.'

'I see you're convinced he'll try again.'

'Can you tell me what's to stop him?'

'No. So let's consider it on that basis.' Charles Russell turned to Lord Normer, the fourth man present. 'D'you think they would plant a second bomb? Out in the sea where it could leak but we couldn't recover it?'

'No, I do not,' Lord Normer said shortly.

'You sound very sure.'

'I am.' Normer looked at the chairman. 'Have they ever acquired a bomb of yours?'

'I'm happy to say they haven't. An Air Force life-raft, I'll own to that. But a bomb they haven't got and they never will.'

'Then it isn't a starter since they'd have to use one of their own. I realize they could dump it where we can't for the moment recover it, but there'd be no guarantee that in a year's time we couldn't and there are underwater cameras of considerable efficiency. Once it was established that any bomb in the sea was theirs, not yours, they'd have defeated themselves completely.' Lord Normer shook his enormous head. 'It's out.'

'Then what's on?'

Lord Normer of Nowhere went suddenly crusty. 'Everyone's been talking about deduction except myself, so now I'm entitled to try some.' He'd been collapsed in his chair but now pulled himself upright heavily. 'Anything occur to you about this Press campaign Canning's stoking?'

'Only he's pretty good at it.'

'So good you should watch it carefully. He's been beating the biggest drum that Americans were caught searching, but asked the next question whether he knew if they'd found anything . . . ' Lord Normer paused significantly. 'He's so far said he didn't know. But they must have known from the Deshmukh woman that you did find something and take it away.'

'I follow your line of thought,' the chairman said, 'but not where it leads us. If I'm reading you correctly you're suggesting a possibility. You're saying it's still open to them to plant a bomb in Parke's Combe and pretend it's ours.'

'I am.'

The chairman looked puzzled. 'You've a sharper mind than I have and I'm probably being presumptuous, but wouldn't your own objections still apply? If they dropped one of their own in the sea we might identify it as theirs. Wouldn't that be even easier on the land? Even if they were willing to let us find it and learn things from it.'

'My friend, you wouldn't find it.'

'Why not?'

'*Because they'd fire it.*'

There was a horrified silence but no one protested. Normer wasn't a man you protested to lightly. The chairman said finally: 'It wouldn't be Anglo-American relations which went up with the bang. That could be war.'

'I'm afraid you're misunderstanding me. I'm not suggesting they're total barbarians. You're thinking in megatons— everybody does. But the last I heard you had a tactical warhead down to fifty thousand tons of high explosive. That, if I may remind you, is round about the bomb load of a B.52. But I'd guess you've got lower than that by now, and if you've done it I'm betting they have.'

'I'm not here to contradict you and you're not embarrassing me for figures. So what would be the effect of a tactical weapon in Parke's Combe?'

'The physical effects? Parke's Combe is conveniently isolated. I gather it's pretty narrow and the sides are distinctly steep, so it would break every window for miles around and destroy any building which happened to be near it . . . There aren't any? Good. There might also be minimal fall-out, depending on how the bomb was made, but I don't think the bang itself is particularly relevant. It would be the moral effects which mattered—that you *had* slipped a second and sworn you hadn't, a dangerous one, moreover, which later went off on us British. Any material damage would almost certainly be secondary. They wouldn't need to inflict it and to try would be rather clumsy. Scientists hate looking clumsy— all of them.'

Scobell was asking quietly: 'How would they plant it?'

'It might be possible by air but very risky. An aeroplane might be sighted and it would probably be heard. If I were responsible I'd do it from the sea again.'

There was a silence while the chairman thought it through; he answered at last, not making difficulties but stating the limitations. 'There are things we can do and things which we cannot. Next time it won't be some coaster and a handful of men they've put aboard. I'd use a submarine myself and you can't interfere with warships on mere suspicion. Not a great Power's.'

'We could double the watch and challenge any ship which came near the coast.'

'Running the risk that they'd slip us sometime. In fog——'

'If I might make a suggestion,' Charles Russell said.

'Please do.'

But Lord Normer had risen. 'I'm going,' he said precisely. 'At this point I always do.' The chairman said something deprecatory but Lord Normer had reached the door. 'I never know more than I need to, I like my sleep.' He managed a bow though it hurt his back. 'Gentlemen,' he said, 'Good luck.'

The three men left started talking very quietly. They talked for an hour and the chairman said finally: 'There's a full moon on Thursday. If they come it'll be then.'

The Second Secretary was listening to the Brahms F major but this time he wasn't relaxing. He was far too anxious and far too tense. This was the crisis of his career. It was still Phase Three as he'd always planned it, but Phase Two had failed and the enemy was on notice. He'd referred upwards again as in duty bound and again they'd been brutally frank with him. The prize was still there but the risk had increased enormously. *His* risk. There had been men who had wanted to call it off, the cautious ones, the good steady soldiers, but the others had voted for him and they'd just been a majority. The Second Secretary didn't resent it that they now covered themselves at his expense. He'd grown up in that world and knew no other.

He poured a glass of wine though it wouldn't help. He would have prayed but he had no God, no God but the gods, the imps of fortune. He poured the wine deliberately on the floor. A libation—fates accept it. It was going to be tonight and that was final. The rest was on the indifferent gods' hard knees.

172

In a rare moment of thinking in images Russell had once seen himself as a disillusioned but still determined male caryatid supporting civilized values against conspirators who wished to destroy them. He had suppressed the thought as fanciful and moreover it was inaccurate, for the destroyers who leant their weight against his grey and reverend head were a very mixed bag and as often as not plain stupid. They covered a spectrum of frightening variety, everything from cold-hearted men with an alien Power behind them down to that woman on the radio with the haw-haw voice, the husband of means and the tedious preoccupation with teenage misdemeanour. But whatever protean form the enemy took, the limitations on Russell's action were the same. The Executive wasn't a secret police, and Russell would have resigned at once at the least pressure that it become one. He had been asked more than once to do something unspecified lest the person the Minister had in mind take some action he'd find embarrassing. Russell had always declined and he always would. But let this person do something *dangerous* and the Executive would react at once, outside the law when necessary. It mostly was. But its business was security, not the convenience of the great, and that went for any government be it red or true blue or a washy pink.

That was the premise and limitations followed it logically. Preventive action was out, like preventive war: you'd be simply destroying what you were salaried to defend. So you waited for something to break and you then defended. You defended like hell and by now you'd become quite good at it.

Charles Russell, this morning, was considering his defence. If Lord Normer was right, and so far he'd been predicting with a wholly alarming accuracy, then foreign nationals would be landing on the northern coast of Devon, and they'd be coming from a country which it would be very unwise to affront. To arrest them would be clumsy and to shoot at them quite fatal. The former would blow the story and the latter could lead to war, but Russell wasn't a romantic and he didn't propose to expose himself without proper and adequate cover. He looked at a note which he'd made at the meeting. There'd have to be men with firearms but they'd need to be carefully hidden. And their orders must be mandatory: shoot only if shot at and then with the utmost discretion.

Russell ticked his note and considered the next. He was going to need a scientist and a scientist of a special kind. Not some backroom boy or a whizz-kid with the equations but a technician with special skills. And above all things fast on the job. He ticked this note too—Lord Normer had looked after it. The third point he'd dealt with himself already, motoring to Parke's Combe by night. He knew the layout perfectly now.

And he mustn't forget the Gladstone bag. According to Lord Normer that would carry it quite comfortably.

The four men had landed from two dinghies and done their job. Now they were walking along the floor of Parke's Combe, back to the sea and their waiting boats. Their pace was processional, their air that of men who had finished their work successfully. They wore jerseys and seaman's trousers, their ends tucked into heavy rubber boots of a type not seen in England. They stopped often and listened, taking their time with an arrogant deliberation. They moved slowly under the summer moon and their shadows were squat behind them.

Where the floor of the combe narrowed two men stepped from nowhere and barred their path. They were breathing a little heavily for they'd had to move fast and silently through the trees which flanked the strangers' route. Russell's heart missed a beat as he stepped into the moonlight. He wasn't frightened but had the needle and the sensation was almost pleasurable. You could never be sure what those others would do. The sensible orders would be those he had given himself, to fire only if fired upon, to resist only if apprehended. Still, you could never be sure. Russell looked at Dominy beside him. His presence was unnecessary, indeed he was breaking orders. Charles Russell hid an affectionate smile. At least he'd been useful to tote the bag.

The leader saw them and held his hand up, and the three men behind him stopped in file. What he saw in the moonlight was two unarmed men, or if they were armed they hadn't drawn. One was elderly but upright still, the other considerably younger. The younger was holding a Gladstone bag.

The officer considered it. His party was armed and it was four men to two, but the officer wasn't stupid. The two men in his path had a confidence he recognized. They wouldn't be alone. The walls of the combe were steep and wooded, perfect cover for the gunners they'd be concealing. It was something out of the text books, the perfect ambush. A single burst could wipe them out and it wouldn't be a single burst. It could turn into a massacre and he had strict orders to avoid one. Nevertheless he wasn't a coward and by now he was very angry. He could read the situation and it was clear that they'd had forewarning. Which meant that in any language known he'd failed and failed disastrously. What was more they were going to humiliate him, a story in those clubs of theirs, laughter to warm their winters . . .

On a reflex he reached for his gun and drew and a single shot broke his elbow. He dropped the gun but he didn't utter.

Charles Russell hadn't moved but now he did. He took the bag from Martin Dominy and walked stiffly towards the officer. Carrying it without Martin's help the bag seemed suddenly much heavier. He put it at the officer's feet, spoke politely but not in English.

'I think you left something behind you.'

A man in the officer's party began to speak but he checked

him sharply. He looked at Charles Russell with naked hate but he kept his voice conversational.

'And now?'

'Kindly open that bag.'

The officer did so left-handed.

'Your property?'

'It was.'

'It is again. Your boats haven't been interfered with and we'll have the pleasure of escorting you.'

Russell turned on his heel and began to walk and the officer smiled faintly. This was balm to his wound and he wasn't thinking about his elbow. Inescapably he'd been bested but he'd been spared the final ignominy. It had been done by an enemy but he was certainly an officer. No guns in his ribs while his own men stared, no unnecessary loss of face, of the authority which this Englishman had recognized. Only a broken arm which didn't count.

They walked to the beach in single file the officer's arm dangling. One of his men had made a sling but he waved it aside impatiently. He was staring approvingly at the sides of the combe . . . They were admirably hidden. Once he thought he'd seen a gunbarrel glint but he wouldn't have cared to swear to it.

At the beach they embarked with the Gladstone bag, two men to each dinghy. As they began to paddle Charles Russell took his hat off. The officer said formally:

'I cannot return the courtesy.'

'I accept the word for the deed. Good bye.'

They began to row strongly, the officer using a single arm. Russell and Martin Dominy watched the dinghies fade in the night haze. Their outlines went first but the moon showed a phosphorescent patch where the oars dipped and rose in a steady rhythm. Russell couldn't see the submarine though he'd been informed about her presence. A couple of miles offshore, submerged, and she'd surface to pick up the dinghies.

Another man had joined them now, and for the first time Martin Dominy spoke.

'You were pretty damned quick.'

'I had to be.'

'A type you knew?'

'No, brand new.' The scientist added wistfully: 'If I were a spy I could ask a million.'

'The casing wasn't difficult?'

'I killed the fuse and the casing, since you call it that, was jam.'

'You made up the weight?'

'Yes, we'd thought of that.'

'And the bits that matter?'

'Well on the way to London now. The helicopter was up on the cliff.'

CHAPTER SEVENTEEN

Charles Russell had been talking to his Minister again. He was indifferent to praise or blame except from a man he sincerely respected, and his Minister was one of those he did. Russell was purring contentedly, for his Minister had stroked his ears with skill. How agreeable, the great man had said, to deal with a practical man for once, how agreeable, he had also implied, to be shot of the lawyers and doctrinaires. The Rule of Law? But of course—it was fundamental. But there was an important if nice distinction between the Rule of Law and the rule of the lawyers. There was still a picturesque functionary called the Lieutenant of the Tower, and part of his ancient duties was taking charge of all prisoners of traitorous intent. Intent. That was no doubt important to a man in Charles Russell's position.

. . . Where were we? Ah yes. There was nothing more disastrous than rushing about in circles getting busy prematurely, and in matters between major Powers the propensity could be fatal. Russell wouldn't be where he was if he didn't know that, but even the most experienced official could be forgiven for yielding to the pressure of extreme events. Colonel Russell had not done so and the Minister was much obliged. Looked at with hindsight the possibilities had been shattering but there'd been masterly inactivity till the moment came round to be active. The words were a cliché but not the less true for that, and if there were any small token of gratitude and a real respect, a knighthood, say, or a really good dinner . . .

Charles Russell had chosen the dinner at once.

He had another good reason this morning to feel well used, for he had just returned from a trip to Burke Hoe where a pair of loose ends had demanded attention. The first had been Bridget Deshmukh and he'd been confident he could handle her. And not without reason. He'd told her as much as he'd dared, then he'd waited for her to react to it. She mightn't be very clever, he'd thought, but she was clearly a sensible woman. She asked him at length:

'You're telling me I'm in danger still?'

'It would be convenient to tell you that but it wouldn't be very truthful. But I'm making a proposition just the same.'

She said unexpectedly: 'I can see I've been a nuisance. Do you want me to leave the Party?'

'Good Heavens, no.' But he knew she would. She wouldn't go out with drums and banners, nobody did unless they meant to write a book on it, but she'd drift away quietly like thousands of others. The yearly rate of wastage wasn't something the Party published. 'Good Heavens, no,' he said again, 'but I'd like you to go away for a while. Just to let the dust settle. You follow me?'

She nodded placidly, making it easy. 'I suppose you could make me anyway . . . Where to?'

'Back to where we both came from. If you agree I could fix the whole thing. I've friends there still, relations really. I should know you weren't in difficulties and they'd be delighted to put you up.'

'They'd be much too grand for me,' she said.

'Oh no, they wouldn't. They've been there as long as you, you know. Just because I work here, just because I don't talk like a music-hall Irishman . . . ' He left it unfinished, lighting her cigarette, a cigar himself. 'Wasn't your name Macnamee?'

She nodded.

'So was my great-great-grandmother's.'

179

She smiled but was thinking it over. 'And what about my job?'

'They'll keep it open. You're a Sister now, aren't you?'

'I was lucky,' she said.

'That isn't my information nor my forecast for your future, and I've good means of forecasting people's futures. Nobody knows you've had any sort of trouble and now they never will. I'll see to that personally as part of our little bargain. And if you're thinking of David Rees it's a waste of effort. He's too small-time to matter, and in any case we've talked to him. We're good at that sort of talk and you can take it that Rees is frightened stiff. He'll hold his tongue and go on holding it. The man who tried to kill you is dead and now we can mop up his household. There isn't any danger now, but a holiday would be, well, discreet.'

'I'd enjoy a bit of a holiday.'

'Let's say we could both *use* it.' He held out his hand. 'Try to think of me kindly.'

'I didn't take you for an Orangeman.'

'I'm not.'

Russell looked at his diary; he had two more appointments and the first was with James Scobell. His secretary showed him in and Russell asked him blandly:

'Did our chairman have a good flight back?'

'It was very smooth indeed, I hear.' Scobell grinned happily. 'Like everything else. But there'll be a certain amount of finger-crossing for a certain amount of time——'

'Not too long, I should say. Every hour that goes by and it's less likely they'll react. How can they react?'

'You tell me that.'

'When they find that horrible thing is minus its guts? They may have found out on the submarine or they could have carried it all the way home before some boffin took a look at it. I don't think it matters which because there's something called face in either case. It's desperately important when you could look extremely foolish. Tell me, what would *you* do?'

'We'd hold our tongues. We'd have to.'

'I'm inclined to think that so will they.'

Scobell nodded shortly. 'And the guts of that most valuable toy? The agreement was to let us share what your backroom boys discover. Payment for services rendered, you know.'

'I'd double-cross you if I dared. I don't.'

James Scobell chuckled. 'Then that covers the international side, but what about here in England.'

'Fair to middling and getting fairer. Lord Normer was perfectly right. They planned for a steady build-up, increasing pressure. First that life-raft, then the bomb. If those had come off I shouldn't be sitting here talking to you. I shouldn't be allowed to. But without them it was what he called it again, an appalling row which with luck could be smoothed over. The machine has got its teeth in it now and it's efficient in its own strange way.'

'Soft soap?'

'The softest. Carlyon Canning has gone abroad, by the way, and you'll agree that's pretty significant. He wouldn't be taking a holiday if his side of the plan alone were still worth playing. He must have had instructions from higher up.'

'Or perhaps you just quietly eased him out.'

Russell said almost sharply: 'You overestimate my authority and you underestimate my judgement.'

'I beg your pardon for a stupid joke.'

'It wasn't a joke but it wasn't quite stupid either.'

'I think I'm getting the message.'

'Good.'

Russell went to the door with James Scobell, then pressed the intercom for Dominy. He was pleased with Martin Dominy, and for just the same reasons his Minister had been pleased with Russell. He'd done nothing sensational but wasn't paid to act sensationally. Rushing about too busily was the occupational ailment of many operators. The second-class ones. Yes, the boy had done well, he'd be safe to promote one higher and see what happened. He mightn't enjoy more time at a desk but he'd settle to it finally. Of course he'd scored a brace of blacks, the sort which lower down the line would have killed a mere strong-arm's chances. To fall off a rock into the arms of the men you were watching, to get kicked in the crutch by a man ten years older . . . Russell wagged his grey head but more in humour than in anger. Hard men were six a penny but men with disciplined patience almost priceless. He'd permit himself a backhander about the need for regular exercise, but that was as far as he'd go or wished to.

Martin Dominy came in quietly and Russell gave him a glass of sherry. 'I spent yesterday at Burke Hoe on a couple of loose ends. I talked to Bridget and Casilda.'

'I wish you well of the pair of them.' Martin Dominy spoke with feeling but Russell ignored it urbanely. 'I've dealt suitably with Bridget but Casilda was more difficult. She's Tom's widow and we're the Executive. We work in a sort of shadowland and that's the way I like it. She's not the type to talk unwisely, but if a big newspaper got over-curious about that business on the Dipper, say the *Gong* . . . '

'Very awkward indeed.'

'An understatement I can appreciate. So I'm sending her back to Spain.'

Martin looked astonished. 'But the boy. She's determined to bring him up English.'

'Quite so.' Russell stared at the ceiling, then back at Martin Dominy. He was going to be promoted so the more he learnt the better. 'May I ask you how you'd have handled it? You want to get Casilda back to Spain. How do you go about it?'

'We've two obvious levers but only two. We could threaten

to stop her pension or we could talk about an accident which wasn't.'

'And would you use either?'

'I wouldn't.'

'Quite right—nor did I. I got at her through the boy himself. He'll never grow up English if she herself stays in England. She'd half realized that already so I wasn't on quite hopeless ground. So she'll keep him in Spain for a year or two, then send him to school in England. Holidays with herself of course, and the grandparents will keep an eye on him. I've put up her pension to meet the expense and it's lucky her in-laws like her. It won't be very easy for her, but she puts the boy first and always has.'

'Not quite first,' Martin said.

'Yes, I know what you mean, but that debt is paid for ever. She paid it in a Fun Fair with a man called Alex Kaunas. Now she'll marry again, I'm sure of it.'

When Martin had gone Russell picked up the telephone. He rang his favourite restaurant . . . Yes, the table by the arch, please, and there'd be two of them today. His guest was called Lord Normer and in a gentle way they'd be celebrating. Make sure the steak wasn't barley-fed and a bottle of the good Lascombes, the one they kept for the few customers who deserved it.

Perhaps Lord Normer didn't, who swilled bitter by the quart. The extra glasses for Russell then, who could modestly feel he'd earned them.

The Second Secretary was waiting for the final telegram. He'd had one already and it hadn't been reassuring. There'd been a time, he reflected, when it could only have been a labour camp and though matters had changed in style by now they'd changed not at all in essentials. He would have to pay for failure and had always expected to do so. In a way he

183

would have preferred the camp: it would have been certain death but finite. But as policy stood today they could drag it out, play cat and mouse and humiliate you. There were dreadful states in Africa where a man could be posted to rot like an imperialist. Africans were black brothers of course, men in the vanguard of the struggle against whatever was the changing word for the never changing enemy. No doubt. The fact remained that they weren't good material, they were often venal and as Marxists unreliable. A posting to an African state would be a sentence of death by frustration.

A clerk brought in a telegram and he decoded it himself. He was obliged to since the code was his alone. He decoded as he'd been trained to, not trying to read the sense till he had the words. Then he read them and his face set hard. He was a stoical man but this was worse then he'd ever feared . . . Not even to Africa. They'd posted him to Delhi and he was to leave within the week. India . . .

India was the anus of the world, the end of nothing. Why, they weren't even black men.